P9-CJW-582

Sticky Notes
and
Brain Freeze

Written and Illustrated by

ALAN SILBERBERG

ALADDIN

NEW YORK LONDON TORONTO SYDNEY

MILO
Sticky Notes
and
Brain Freeze

ALADDIN

An imprint of Simon & Schuster Children's Publishing Division

1230 Avenue of the Americas, New York, NY 10020

First Aladdin hardcover edition September 2010

Designed by Karin Paprocki

The text of this book was set in Minister Book.

Manufactured in the United States of America 0810 FFG

2 4 6 8 10 9 7 5 3 1

Library of Congress Cataloging-in-Publication Data

Silberberg, Alan.

Milo : sticky notes and brain freeze / by Alan Silberberg. — 1st Aladdin hardcover ed.

p. cm.

Summary: In love with the girl he sneezed on the first day of school and best pals with Marshall, the "One Eyed Jack" of friends, seventh-grader Milo Cruikshank misses his mother whose death has changed everything at home.

Cartoon illustrations interspersed throughout story.

ISBN: 978-1-4169-9430-5 (hardcover)

[1. Grief—Fiction. 2. Death—Fiction. 3. Mothers—Fiction. 4. Friendship—Fiction.] I. Title.

PZ7.S5798Mi 2010

[Fic]—dc22

2010012708

ISBN 978-1-4424-0942-2 (eBook)

For my mom

Sticky Notes and Brain Freeze

gesundheit

SUMMER GOODMAN NEVER KNEW WHAT hit her. That's because it was me, and as soon as I collided with her in the hallway—scattering every one of her perfectly indexed index cards—I disappeared into the mob of kids who'd arrived to help realphabetize her life.

I love Summer Goodman but she barely knows I exist, which I'm pretty okay with because when you love someone, they don't have to do anything—and Summer does nothing, so I think it's all going to work out great.

One possible problem is, I've never actually spoken to Summer, except the time I said "sorry," which was after I sneezed on the back of her neck the first day in science class.

It was a really wet one—and she didn't sneeze back on me or have me suspended, so that's just another reason I think she's so great.

What isn't so great is that I'm the "new kid" again, which isn't as bad as it sounds unless you think about how awful it is. That's why I put all my focus on the more important stuff, like Summer Goodman and how my germs have actually bonded directly onto her skin!

The way I see it, surviving this year is all I have to do. Start to finish in one whole piece and then I win. Of course, being me, winning doesn't come easy, which is why I created an alias, a supercool guy who will step in when I mess up or can't talk or both.

Dabney St. Claire is mysterious, smart, and popular without even trying. I talk to him out loud sometimes, but mostly he's just in my head, along for the ride, telling me how he'd do what I'm doing, only without doing it so wrong.

My sister thinks there's something the matter with me, which is why she tells her friends I have a metal plate in my head, which would actually be a cool thing because then I would never have to fly on airplanes because my skull would set off alarms. Her friends always look at me with sad puppy-dog eyes, and even though I don't have a metal plate or even a *paper plate* in my head, I stare back at them and speak my favorite language: SAPTOGEMIXLIKS.

This is just another reason my sister wants to move again.

*TRANSLATION: My sister eats her fingernails and sleeps with a teddy bear named Snuggy.

name game

MOVING IS SOMETHING I AM ACTUALLY good at, and I don't mean in the "get down and boogie" kind of way. I'm what my mom called an "A-1 Klutz King," which is why I crash into things (like Summer

Goodman) and trip off of curbs a lot. I guess it's a skill or maybe a defective gene that is slowly mutating inside of me. The only good news is that Dabney St. Claire is smooth on his feet ALL THE TIME, so I know there's hope.

My latest house is 22 Marco Place and it's the fifth house I've ever lived in.

Seeing how I'm almost thirteen years old, that means I move about once every 2.5 years. I'm sure there are kids who move a lot more than that, and I know some kids still live in the houses they were born in and I bet they get to live in those houses forever and get buried in the backyard with all their cats and dogs and turtles (R.I.P.).

The best part of moving a lot is you get good at the worst part, which is the packing and unpacking. The reason I'm *super*good at this is that after the last two moves I figured out all I had to do was pack and unpack one box and leave the other seven in my closet.

My one box is labeled ESSENTIALS and has all my best stuff in it, including but not limited to: books; action figures; signed arm cast from when I fell off the swing and my mom drew a picture of the Hulk on it, which looked more like a huge sick frog, but it was the thought that counted and I still have it.

The other boxes . . . I've actually forgotten what's in them. So I guess whatever's inside isn't that important anymore. Lots of stuff isn't important anymore, but that's just the way it is.

One thing about a new school is they always mess up your name so that by the end of your first week no one has a clue who you really are. To be honest, getting called the wrong name is one thing that I actually like. Bob. Steve. Rick. Those are the kind of names that put you smack in the middle of the Cool Name Club.

When you have a Cool Name Club name, it doesn't even matter what you look like. You just know you're destined for GREAT things, like

Student Council or the lead in the school play, which hopefully is *not* a musical because no matter what name you have, you're still an A-1 Klutz King!

But Milo Cruikshank is not the name of the guy

who plays Macbeth. That's the name of a kid who *maybe* gets to help out backstage and just gets in the way and probably doesn't even get his name in the program. Milo Cruikshank is a loser name, which is obviously why it belongs to me.

My dad is always trying to get me on the "same page" with the whole "Life Changes" thing, which makes no sense to me. If you're supposed to accept that life is always changing and be fine that today may be okay but tomorrow might be the worst day in your life—EVER—then how do you do your homework? Why do you brush your teeth? And who's going to be there in the kitchen to make you pancakes and let you have a tiny sip of coffee (with tons of milk)?

But life does change, which is why I'm so glad

that I love Summer because she is part of the "good" changes and not the "bad" ones that follow me around like shadows.

I first saw Summer Goodman even before school started. It was August and we'd just moved into House #5. She was buying gum at the Pit Stop down the street, which is one of those mini-mart places that sells pretty much everything, like bread and milk and car air fresheners shaped like pine trees, which is so stupid because they don't smell like any tree I've ever smelled—they smell like dog pee, so if you need one of those to make your car smell *better*, I'd hate to know what it smelled like before.

We needed toilet paper for the new house, and since my sister gets to sleep late just because she's a "teenager," my dad made me walk to the Pit Stop for an emergency T.P. run.

Now, if you ever plan to meet the most pretty girl in your whole life, there's two things you don't want:

One: You don't want to have one of those haircuts your dad gives you because he owns the dullest pair of scissors in the world.

And two: You don't want to be holding a jumbo twelve-pack of two-ply super-soft toilet paper!

NOTHING could be more embarrassing . . . unless you forget to wear pants, which luckily I did not.

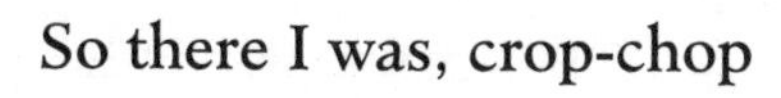

So there I was, crop-chop haircut and hiding behind a mountain of toilet paper, when Summer Goodman first walked into my life. Seeing her actually made my heart beat faster, which is cliché and stuff, but that's how pretty she was in her white shorts and tank top. Her hair was the color of lemonade, and I don't mean the pink kind.

She walked straight to the candy rack, grabbed a pack of Strawberry Squirt bubble gum, and went right past me to the counter to pay. She looked at me just once, which again makes me want to say: Why toilet paper? Why didn't we need something cool, like laundry soap or a fishing license?

Anyway, Summer Goodman looked right at me and said the six best words I've ever heard in my life: "That stuff really is supersoft."

And then she was gone, and I knew this was going to be the best move we ever made.

missing

HAT DO I MISS?

I miss laughing.

I miss orange peels.

I miss staying home from school just because she says it's okay.

I miss a dinner table that doesn't feel lopsided and a kitchen that's full of her.

How do you know that every day is the last chance to fill up on the good stuff; to jam-pack your pockets with a whole life's worth of everything you're going to miss forever?

"When you don't have something anymore, you learn to live without it." That's what my dad told me that first night after he found me sleeping inside a closet underneath a pile of my mom's clothes. All the different smells of her were still there and the memories were alive even if she wasn't.

I looked up into his face and wondered why would I ever want to learn to live without her? That felt like she really would be gone forever, and I wanted to limp on the broken piece of me so I could feel her there all the time.

But I didn't say anything to my dad. I just let him lift me up and hold me close to him and I felt him breathe her in too. And we stayed that way for a long time, both frozen in the smells of what life was like before the fog swallowed us whole.

reset button

STARTING OVER IS LIKE HITTING THE reset button on a game that makes you lose all your points and wipes out any of the good stuff you've spent hundreds of hours learning, like how to navigate the slime chasm and beat Level 8, where the only way to survive the dragon's breath is to use the invisible lava rocks and *not* your lasers.

Being in a new house means I had to go to another new school. There was no way around it. I was starting over all over again.

It wasn't like I didn't do everything I could to get out of it, like trying really hard to stop time so I could stay in my pajamas forever. But apparently, time doesn't stop unless you take out the battery from the kitchen clock, which your dad figures out and just replaces.

My dad's eyes roll up into his head a lot, and that is what happens when I tell him about my new plan: homeschooling. Apparently, there are millions of kids who get to go to school in their houses, and I am sure this means they sleep until ten and then watch the Discovery Channel until lunch, which I bet is a quick drive to a fast-food place. Homeschool sounds like my kind of place, especially because my bed is so soft, and so that's what I debate with my dad for two hours and

fifteen minutes without a single bathroom break.

The answer is the same as if I hadn't argued at all: "Milo, I know it's tough, but you have to go to school."

Sigh. So that's the way it is—I have to start over. Again. Only this time it isn't just any kind of school, it's *junior high school*. Seventh grade. This time hitting that reset button and losing all my points won't make a difference because junior high school is a whole new game.

My first day at the new school, the one called Forest Grove Junior High, I did everything right, and by "right" I mean the way Dabney St. Claire told me: Keep my eyes straight ahead and stay out of trouble.

Of course, Dabney St. Claire doesn't have to worry about getting lost looking for the one boys' bathroom that the kid named Mikey Guzzman says is the "safe" one. And Dabney St. Claire knows nothing about standing in the wrong lunch line because you are paying with *real* money and not some electronic card that is what the line you've been standing in for twenty minutes is for!

The day lasts forever, starting with the formalities of sitting in the office where no one knows where to put me, which is pretty great because I missed two whole periods and one of them was gym.

Finally, a boy who I swear smelled like a can of cat food had been rubbed all over his body shows up and simply says, "Follow me." And then he silently leads me down the empty hallway where kids inside classes watch us through their open doors as if I am being escorted to the electric chair.

"You'll like it here," Cat Food Boy says as he picks his nose. "Everyone does."

But what he doesn't know—what I know too

well—is that I'm not like "everyone." I'm much more of a "no one" kind of guy, so I know right away that the chances of me liking Forest Grove are like a million to zip.

And then—just before we turn the corner to go up to the second floor where my locker is—I see her, the pretty girl from the Pit Stop, sitting perfectly in her front-row chair looking out the door at Cat Food Boy and me. I want to wave but my arms are too full with all the books they've given me; so I smile instead, and this is how cool she is: She doesn't smile back. Awesome!

"Hey," I say to this boy who really needs a bath or new laundry soap, one made from smells that are not pet food. "That girl back there. Do you know her?"

He tosses a look behind us. "Sure. Summer Goodman. Everyone knows her."

And that is all the information I need, because up until that moment I had no idea who the girl I saw at the Pit Stop was, but from that moment on I had her name and the knowledge that EVERYONE knows her—and I make up my mind that this school year I will become an "everyone" and leave the "no one" me behind in the dust.

The rest of that first day is a blur of kids moving full speed ahead while I bump along in the breakdown lane. My schedule is pretty full and there aren't nearly enough slots on my sheet that say *Do Nothing.* English. Gym. Geography. Math. Art. Science. Spanish. Health. Suddenly the school year looks like a highway that is going to stretch on and on without any exit ramps—just lots of homework.

Another bell rings, and I just shrug because I know I'm late for something . . . but I also know I can use the "new kid" excuse at least for a few days.

"You're Milo." This comes from a girl to my left, and since I don't know her, I decide to play it cool in case she is some sort of spy and wants to steal my locker combination, which luckily for me, I have already forgotten. "You live on my street." She keeps walking with me even though I am now doing my double-time quick walk. "Next door, actually. Weird, huh?"

Now, lots of things in life are weird:

But the fact that this girl lives in a house that happens to be next door to mine just doesn't hold a candle to something *totally* weird, like a guy who can hammer nails into his nose.

I don't say any of this to her. I just stop walking

and nod and say, "Yeah. Really weird." And then we both just stand there.

Whole minutes go by, and we're still just standing in the empty hallway not talking. Of course, if this is some sort of test, there is no hope she can win because if she thinks she can outmute me, she is in for one big surprise. Not saying stuff is one contest where I know I am the king.

"Okay then," she says. "See ya around."

And then she walks off and I am free, and the sweat on my upper lip and I breathe a sigh of relief until I hear the sound of someone running, and I don't even dare look around because I am 53 percent sure those footsteps belong to her.

"Sorry. I forgot to tell you my name."

I don't have it in me to tell her I really don't care, so instead I use my *mind-control powers* to convince her to just leave me alone.

Apparently, my brain is not up to the task because she keeps talking.

"Hillary Alpert," she says, thrusting her hand out at me like it's one of those levers you pull on a slot machine. "Next-door neighbor extraordinaire!"

Stuck in the hallway, with no escape in sight, I give her a real look-over and notice her skinny legs look like tent poles. Her smile is like a curly French fry, and her eyes are brown and wide and seem to stay open all the time. And there's a smell I pick up that is definitely gum-related. Maybe watermelon.

"Well?" she says with her slot-machine hand just waiting for me to try my luck. "What do you say?"

And though I say nothing, I stick out my hand

and we shake two quick times before she zips off to wherever a girl like that goes—which hopefully is not where I am going, which is science.

The good news about that first day is I learned one great thing: Summer Goodman is the name of the prettiest girl I'd ever seen. Also important, but way less exciting, I learned that I will probably never understand Spanish, and that even after asking the janitor for help, I still can't get my locker open.

The bad news about my first day has to do with the girl with the watermelon smell. By the time I got home, there was a purple note taped to our front door that read *Nice to meet ya, Milo!!* And it was signed with *her* name.

i hate leprechauns

HOUSE #5 ISN'T BAD. IT DOESN'T HAVE the secret stink that House #3 had so already that's a plus.

I have my own room this time, which means my sister has less to bug me about. Three houses ago ("The Apartment of Endless Stairs") we had to share a room, and she actually painted a line down the middle and labeled all the things I could touch, which, seeing as I was farther from the door, meant that the trash basket and my own bed were pretty much the only things I could lay a finger on.

Since the light switch was on her side of the room, I was stuck in the dark a lot more than I would've liked, but I used a flashlight to read and go to the bathroom and one time used it to whack my sister on the knee because she said I had to hold my breath for the rest of the night because

Guess MY ½ of the ROOM

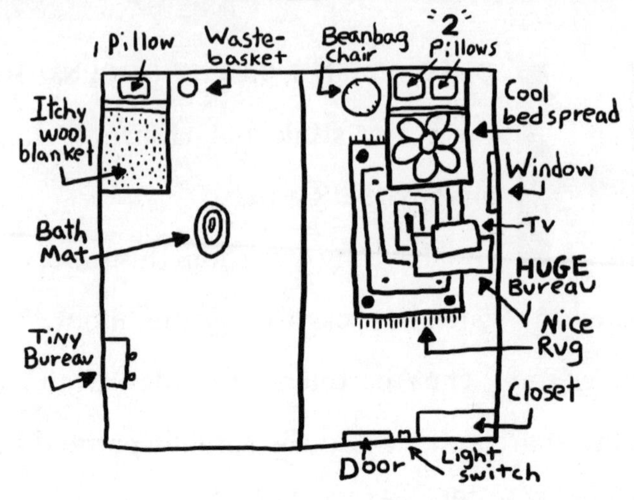

I'd accidentally breathed "her air," and even I knew you can't divide air. After that I didn't have a flashlight anymore, but we moved to House #4 a month later, and then nothing really mattered much and definitely not a stupid flashlight!

House #4 is the Fog House because when I think back to that house, that's what I feel like in my brain. Everything gets all gray and cloudy, and even though it was probably the nicest-looking house, it'll always be a blurry, fog-filled place to me—the house where everything went from one thing . . . to another.

In Life that's what happens: Things start off as ONE THING, then become SOMETHING ELSE.

- TADPOLES become FROGS.

- MAGGOTS become FLIES.

- BICYCLES left out in the rain for two months

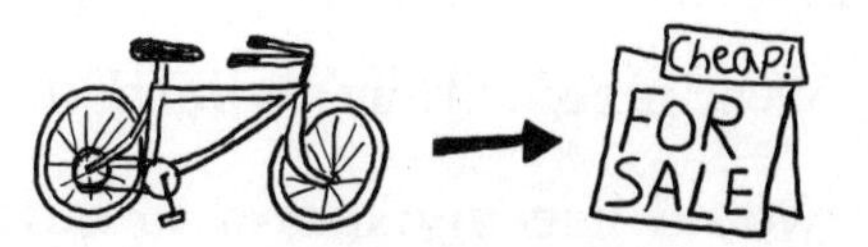

  become FOR SALE items (and you get only ten bucks for yours because of all the rust *and* because someone stole both tires!).

Before the Fog House, I was one thing. But *after* the Fog House . . . well, I'm still not sure what I've become.

Summer Goodman lives in an awesome house, and I'm sure there isn't a pinch of fog anywhere even close to it. I don't know how many times she's moved because maybe you don't remember, but I don't really talk to her that much or actually ever.

Hillary Alpert, I have to talk to mainly because she lives next door, rides the same school bus, and also likes to eat Lucky Charms cereal without the magical marshmallow bits.

When I was little, I really believed the leprechaun on TV when he said that the marshmallow charms were magic. That's when I stopped eating them and would use my spoon to quickly herd the charms all up and scoop them to safety before my mom dumped on the milk. Then I'd run up to my room and add them to my secret stash of clovers, moons, hearts, and that other shape inside my money box, which looked and smelled like it used to be full of cigars.

I really believed those shapes were magically

magic and not just magically *delicious* (which they weren't!). Every couple days or so I'd take a few out and try to wish for stuff—like a dog, or a new action figure, or one time I tried to turn my sister into an ant so I could step on her and say, *Hey squirt, how does that feel, huh?*

After my mom first got sick, I used them a lot. Every day I'd try a new shape. Or a combination of shapes. And then no shapes at all.

I found out those charms weren't magic or lucky. They were just stale candy, and I gave up on magic after flushing my secret box of charms down the toilet. And because I saw through the leprechaun's lies, I decided from that moment on to eat only the cereal flakes and let those stupid shapes drown in the milk and get all soggy and worthless, which is exactly what they are!

Hillary Alpert never told me why *she* doesn't eat the marshmallow bits. Maybe she has a relative who choked on a clover and had to have an emergency operation, which would definitely explain why someone else would steer clear of the things.

As next-door neighbors go, Hillary is kind of a pain—except for the fact that she knows where Summer Goodman lives. The way she tells it, one time she went to Summer's house when they both took gymnastics together a zillion years ago. Hillary says Summer was lousy at gymnastics, but I think Hillary is just saying that to make up for the fact that Summer was probably the best in the class.

Anyway, Hillary wrote down Summer's address, and that's how I know she lives at the very top of

this huge hill called Salisbury Street, which is totally impossible to bike all the way up so you push your bike most of the way while walking out of breath behind it. Once at the top of Salisbury Street (and once you catch your breath), it's so clear that Summer's house is the one with flowers planted along the whole front yard. And even though I just mainly ride my bike back and forth past her house after school and on the weekends, and sometimes stop across the street and watch the place from behind some bushes just to make sure there aren't signs of trouble, I can tell it's a great place to live and I bet Summer has the best bedroom there.

I can't wait to tell Summer how fantastic her house is—once we get past the awkward phase of our relationship, which I hope will be before eighth grade or before I have to move again. And just to give that hope an extra little push, I break down and sneak a pink marshmallow heart from my cereal bowl and make the tiniest whisper-wish ever . . .

. . . that Summer Goodman speaks to me soon.

one-eyed jacks

THE PHONE DOESN'T RING MUCH, AND when it does, it's pretty much a safe bet that it isn't ringing for me. I don't believe in text messages or IMs or even e-mail, and if I had a cell phone, you can be sure I'd never respond back to any of that stuff! If you want to talk to someone, you should just call them up or knock on their door or sit on your bike across the street and wait to just say hi.

Anyway, when the phone rings and it is a person calling me, it's one of two people.

IT'S EITHER:

Hillary Alpert, who wants to know what homework there is or if maybe I want to walk next door and watch a TV show at her house, which is dumb because she knows I have a TV in my house.

OR IT'S:

Marshall Hickler, who calls pretty much because he wants to, not because his mother is whispering in the background, *"Because he's new here and he's had a tough time and you're going to be nice to him."*

If friends were playing cards, Marshall Hickler would be a Jack. No. Not just a Jack—he'd be a *One-Eyed* Jack because those are cooler and much more special than regular Jacks. Marshall isn't an Ace or a King or a Queen because Aces don't have a face, and Kings think they're too good for the room, and Queens . . . well, come on, they're girls!

"One-Eyed Jack" is what I call him sometimes, and even though he doesn't know why I do that, he doesn't even care because "One-Eyed Jack" is way better than what other kids call him: "Marsh Mouth," "Hickey Hickler" and a few other names that are really mean and nowhere near as super-great as "One-Eyed Jack."

Marshall doesn't live next door like Hillary, but he does ride the same bus as me, which is how we met the day we both had to sit in the same seat—the one that some girl named Martha Vidwicki kinda barfed on. I mean, the barf was long gone but it was still the last seat left (due to the leftover smell), and since Marshall gets on a few stops before me, he had already bitten the bullet and decided to sit there. That's why when I got on and saw that the only empty seat was next to the kid with the funny teeth, I didn't care one bit if it reeked a little because he gave me the head nod, and even I know that meant it was okay to sit there.

Sitting side by side on the smelly seat, I noticed he was wearing a Space Gizmoid T-shirt, which is probably the best video game in the history of forever. And right then I knew here was a kid who just might pass my friend test.

MY FRIEND TEST

Answer YES or NO to the following:

1) Have you ever secretly wished you were someone else?

(yes ❑ no ❑)

2) Do you dream in color? (yes ❑ no ❑)

3) Can you eat your weight in any food? (yes ❑ no ❑)

If YES, what food is it? ______________________

4) Have you ever been convicted of a crime?

(yes ❑ no ❑)

To be honest, the only question that matters is the last one because it would be pretty hard for me to hang out with a real-life criminal, even if he had his own satellite TV in his bedroom or a swimming pool. Luckily, Marshall's never been to prison, and he answered all the questions without laughing or punching my shoulder, which I'm pretty sure is slightly deformed probably from being punched so often by kids who didn't make the cut.

So now when the phone rings and it isn't for my sister and it isn't my aunt checking up on my dad and it's not Hillary Alpert wanting to know what channel her favorite TV show is on (like I care), it's Marshall Hickler, and it's a call just for me.

Here's how Marshall and I talk:

"Hey."

"Hey."

(Pause.)

"Whatcha doin'?"

"Not much. You?"

(Pause.)

"Nothin'."

(The pauses are okay because neither Marshall nor I worry that the other one is using the blank spaces to think of a way to tell the other one what a loser he is.)

"You wanna meet at the Pit Stop? Grab a Freezie?"

"I guess."

We go our different ways to arrive at the Pit Stop, and one of us or the other buys two Freezies, and hopefully the lime syrup is not empty because when it is, I suffer through the cherry, which to be honest, just tastes like old cough medicine. Then we sit outside and sip the icy drinks and talk about pretty much anything that pops into our heads or nothing at all, whichever comes first.

Marshall never asks anything that might make me feel bad, and I do my best not to bring up certain stuff too. For instance, his dad doesn't have a job and is hard at work trying to come up with quick ways to get rich. Marshall once had me over to his house, and his dad made us both try this electric pen thing he created using some idea he said he found on the Internet. According to Marshall's dad, his electro-ink invention was going to put them straight on easy street, but all it really did was give my hand a wicked shock and ruin one of my favorite pair of jeans when the thing exploded.

So I don't ask him *How's your dad?* and in return Marshall doesn't ask me anything, which we both agree is pretty much safe territory.

We don't have many classes together (just gym and lunch) but that's okay because no matter what happens between bus rides to and from school, I know I have a friend in One-Eyed Jack.

stuff

I'VE MEMORIZED SUMMER GOODMAN'S SCHOOL schedule and do my best to casually linger near the places she might happen to be. Through careful planning, my goal is to be in the "vicinity" of Summer but not *next* to her or even within direct eye shot. I also ride my bike past her house as often as possible.

Even though we've been in school only a few weeks, I've mapped our whole relationship out and see exactly how Summer and I are going to celebrate our monthly anniversaries. Of course, all this depends on my talking to her, which I have faith will definitely happen sooner than later because I'm practicing every night in the mirror.

Dabney St. Claire says that "timing is everything," which is why I make sure to wear a watch every day so I'm always ready *just in case*. I figure

Anniversary BLING

1 MONTH

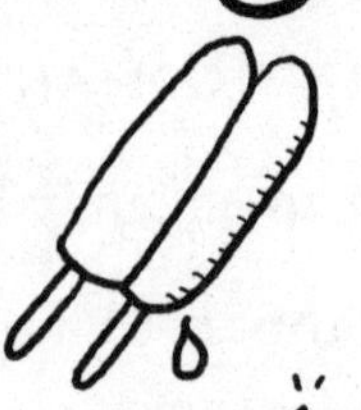

Popsicles – the kind with 2 sticks. Hopefully grape or cherry!

2 MONTH

Movie Passes (probably not good on weekends or at special screenings)

3 MONTH

My Sister's iPod – as soon as she forgets to take it with her!

4 MONTH

Romantic Dinner (at her house – where her MOM makes us something without peppers 'cuz they give me gas)

5 MONTH

A RiNG! – so what if it's plastic?

6 MONTH

GETAWAY to Paris or Orlando (Marshall thinks I'm being so unrealistic "it's scary.")

it's like when you go to a baseball game and bring your glove because it's *possible* a foul ball will come right at you. And even though you're sitting under the grandstand roof where no balls ever go, you wear that baseball glove through the whole game, which makes the popcorn you buy taste like dirt and oil and other stuff you can't even put a finger on—but probably already did—and all that matters is you feel ready for the slimmest-ever chance that the first stray ball in the history of baseball is going to be hit right at your impossible seats.

Marshall tells me I'm dreaming, but what does he know? He's never been in love with anyone but his dog, and dogs don't know any better than to love you back—so where's the effort there?

So until my perfect plan gets the chance to be executed, and by "executed," I mean "activated," not "killed off"—though when you think about it, maybe that would be a better use of the word—anyway, until that moment arrives when Summer Goodman

and I hold actual hands and not ones that I draw on an empty page in my notebook . . . until then I keep busy and do what I always do. Stuff.

STUFF #1:

When my mom was sick, I got to watch as much TV as I wanted as long as I didn't have homework, which is so stupid because even if I did have homework, I would never tell anyone and they were all too busy and worried to notice that all I did was come home from school and turn on the tube and grab a bowl of ice cream.

These days my dad doesn't care what I watch or how much or when. So I make sure to keep the remote by my side at all times, and if I were a cowboy, it would be TV remotes in my holsters and not guns, which are dangerous in the real way and not in the "TV rots your brain" way.

STUFF #2:

Sometimes when there's nothing on TV, I walk to the end of my street and sit on top of the red and blue mailbox and watch cars. It's a pretty busy street—the kind with a stoplight and a bus route—so there's always some traffic to look at. Marshall comes with me sometimes, and sometimes I just do it alone, but either way I do it because of the game I made up, which is pretty simple once you hear the rules:

The Rules: I give myself a limited number of cars, like ten, and then I watch as they drive past me in either direction, and the object of my made-up game is to see if I can pick a car with a perfect family inside that I can have as my own.

It's not as easy as it sounds because (a) sometimes it's just old people or taxicabs or a mom or dad screaming at their kids, so right away you don't want to be in that family! And (b) even when you see a car with the right appearance inside, you only have a second to sum up if they are the family that will make you feel like you belong and tuck you in at night and go to the beach in the summer, where you all bury your dad in the sand and make him look like a mermaid.

And if you can find the perfect family in one of the ten cars (or whatever number you pick), then you WIN and your life can be happy. But if you can't, you go back home and do STUFF #1 until it's time for bed.

Lucky for me I found my...
Lunch Bunch
Gotta get a good table!
Lunch Tray Louie
he'd rather have a good SEAT than a good LUNCH!
What if the mayo in my tuna went bad??
...or my juice box has already expired??
Kevin Mills "MR. WORRY"
has NOT eaten Lunch in 3 MONTHS!
MINE!
Debbie "Dibs" Dinsmore
(never shared food in her life)
I sense feta cheese and ham!
The Salami Swami
Remember- you are WHO you eat with!
...and mac'n'cheese ROCKS!

whack-a-mole

SEPTEMBER IS ALMOST OVER. DABNEY St. Claire says we should celebrate with a cake, but that would mean making one, and I've been banned from baking stuff since the time I thought double-chocolate brownies meant doubling the recipe and the stove kind of erupted.

September used to mean waiting for the leaves to change colors, but now September is the month of new schools and new houses, where old feelings seem to be everywhere. But this September is different because this September includes Summer Goodman. Here is what I know about her so far:

1) She likes Strawberry Squirt bubblegum.
2) She is and/or was a gymnast (better than Hillary!).
3) She lives in a great house at the top of a huge hill.
4) She is liked by everyone but never looks at me.
5) I love her.

Those are the reasons that add up to why surviving this September is a piece of cake (one that I will *not* be baking anytime soon), and if you don't believe me, just look back at my last couple of Summer-less Septembers to see how terrible they both were.

Last September: Well, let's face it—sixth grade and I never quite got along. I stopped counting how many times I went home sick. I stopped doing homework too.

And the September before that was the September right after the fog swooped in and nothing was all right and time felt crooked. It was the first school year I had to start without "her," and I was late a lot and stayed home a lot, and most of the year was a blur because the fog was really thick and there wasn't a single thing that could make it clearer. But this September just *feels* different and I'm getting to be almost okay, and October is so close I can smell it. Dabney St. Claire reminds me: *One school month* almost *down—only nine more to go!*

The cool thing about September is it whizzes by thanks to all the time-wasting activities the school thinks help us kids have a "successful academic year." Unfortunately, the one time-waster I don't like is the "anti-bullying" assembly. It's all so fake. The principal will talk about how awful it is to get picked on and then get really serious and announce, as if it's the end of World War III, *"This school is a No-Bully Zone!"* And then everyone cheers and *hoot-hoots* and all the kids who clearly are the kids who get bullied sit a little taller, and all the kids who do the bullying sit a little lower, and it kind of reminds me of one of those Whack-A-Mole games, only the moles are the kids popping up in their seats, because everyone knows the bullies are just waiting until the assembly is over to whack each mole kid back into feeling scared and lousy.

I don't like bullies, and so it's no surprise that they don't like me. Even after almost one month I know my school has lots of them, and they usually stick out because they are the ones dunking kids' heads in toilets or kicking lockers shut just when you finally figure out how to use your locker combination to get it open.

Anyway, like I said before, September is nearly over, and I accomplished two amazing things: I am in love with Summer Goodman; and I have a real friend named One-Eyed Jack. Also, I am pretty sure I am already failing two subjects, but everyone knows you never need math and who cares about gym?

Lucky for me, there are plenty of things a kid can become without excellent math skills, and that's exactly what I say to my dad when the letter shows up telling him I *really* need extra help or else I'll flunk.

"I need this like I need a hole in my head," my dad says as he puts the letter down on the table and then puts his own head in his hands, and I feel really sorry I am so much of a mess-up.

"I can do better," I lie. "I'll do hypnosis."

Hypnosis worked before when he wanted to quit smoking, so why wouldn't it help me figure out if $x = 10$, what is y? Besides, I secretly want to let some hypno-guy, who probably has a glass eye and a pet monkey, put me into a trance with his swinging watch.

And maybe while I'm under his control getting all those math secrets rewired in my head he can also help me stop thinking of all the bad stuff. Maybe hypnotizing me will make the Fog House go away, and then I can be like everyone else, and Summer Goodman will go to the movies with me and actually know my name.

Even though I think this is a good idea—I've watched enough cartoons to know that hypnotizing someone is great for making them quack like a duck every time someone says the word "pastrami"—but it isn't a magic cure for anything real, unless it's smoking, in which case it totally rocks, even though my dad still sneaks a cigarette or two when he thinks my sister and I aren't looking.

I leave him in the living room just staring at the letter and go up to sit on my bed in my room, where I can shut the door and not let anything in. I know it's just stupid math, but I also know my dad is downstairs hating me, and suddenly September—which is almost over—is a really hard month all over again, and I really, *really* wish my mother were here to tell me it doesn't matter.

But she's not here, and it does matter, and I want to climb inside myself and hide but instead I just turn off the light and lie on top of my bed and wonder if Dabney St. Claire ever has any problem figuring out what *x* and *y* really are.

my dad

(Sitting on the front steps)

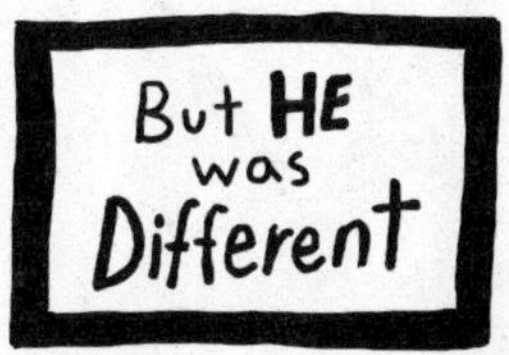

...and I wonder where my REAL dad went– and I hope he's Okay 'cuz I MISS HIM as much as I MISS HER.

egghead

MR. SHIVNESKY'S BALD HEAD IS THE reason math and I do not get along.

I know I can't blame my teacher's scalp for my awful grade, which is wavering between a C and an F but is really a D-minus.

The real problem with Mr. Shivnesky's head is that he isn't bald in the "*oh no*, there's nothing I can do about it" kind of way. He's bald in the worst way ever.

The ON PURPOSE way.

He shaves his head, and I know because when you pass his desk and he's busy grading papers or flipping through a magazine that he says is all about "education" but sure looks like *People* magazine to me, if you look down at his head, you can see it's got a five-o'clock shadow like my dad's face. Then the next day you walk by his head and he's *obviously* just shaved and shined it, and unless he's doing this for some medical reason or national security, I think Mr. Shivnesky needs to stop making his head look like a bowling ball, and if he has to, he can borrow a baseball hat from Pete down at the Pit Stop, who I know has more than one.

I think when you do something on purpose that other people do without even trying, then it's kind of like cheating on a test, and that is something, no matter how bad my grade might be, I would never ever do.

See, unlike Mr. Shivnesky, the people who are *really truly* bald have no choice of hairstyles and probably feel really bad about how they look in family photos or on the JumboTron screen at major sporting events.

Those people are bald because that's just the way the DNA dice rolled out.

But other people—they're bald because maybe they got sick and had to have medicine that made their hair fall out, and then you never know if you should knock real softly and ask if they want juice or if you should maybe just stay downstairs watching TV with the sound so low that you don't know what's happening on your favorite show . . .

and for the first time in your life that's pretty much okay.

Those people have no hair and have no choice about it, and they have to wear wigs or floppy hats, or some days when they don't care, they just walk around the house in their bathrobe, bald as the eggs inside the fridge.

One day we all sat in the kitchen and drew faces on hard-boiled eggs so that the whole family could be bald together. My sister made a paper crown for my mom's egg, and I drew a bow tie and goofy glasses on mine, and my mom laughed a lot, which made me feel great, especially when she decided that all four of our eggs were at a big fancy party. And so we all made our eggs dance around the table.

I tried saving those eggs for a long time by wrapping them in toilet paper and hiding them in my closet, but some things don't last as long as you want them to.

fooling the fog

WAKING UP IS THE HARDEST PART of the day. That's when my "Before" and my "After" get confused which side of the fog they belong on.

It's not quite day yet, and the little light sneaking through my window shade nudges against my eyelids and my brain tries making sense of the bits of dreams and weird thoughts that flash on and off inside my head—and I taste my own bad breath, and then I need to go to the bathroom—and even with my eyes still closed, there's a sound of laughter rising to my room along with the smells of bacon and coffee, and that's when I picture her and know everything is fine, and as soon as I think that, my smile goes bad with the memory of how wrong I am.

I'm in my room. In the bed she never tucked a single sheet into. There are dirty clothes piled everywhere and taped boxes in the closet just waiting to be moved to another house. And I'm alone. And it's just my dad downstairs making another breakfast of oatmeal with raisins. And no matter how hard I try, I can't fall back asleep and find the exact moment she's still here.

top 5

BECAUSE I LIKE TO EAT CHEERIOS ONE "o" at a time I sometimes miss the school bus. When that happens, it means I have to walk to school, which I absolutely *hate* to do mainly because I'm almost positive one leg is shorter than the other and my stride isn't being maximized. I read a story online about a kid whose stride was underused and he had to have six operations just to correct it, so I know I have a good argument here.

That's why on Cheerios days I do my best to make sure I get a ride to school from my dad, who says it's totally inconvenient because it takes him *way* out of his way, but he does it anyway because I think he doesn't want me to have to have all those operations. Part of the problem is that he also drives my sister, which is also out of his way but in the *other* way so I do see his point but don't think it's a good enough reason to get so mad.

My sister goes to the high school, which starts even earlier than my school, so we drop her off first and then it's just him and me and "The Top 5 Topics of Conversation."

As soon as we're alone in the car, my dad starts by picking a question from the list (1–5), and I usually answer it with the shortest response possible. My favorite answers are: "Nope," "Uh-uh," "I dunno," and "Okay." These pretty much cover anything he asks, and sometimes I toss in a "We'll see," just to mix things up.

Depending on traffic and what oldies come on the radio, we usually move through about three or four topics before the ride is over and we both sigh.

I normally don't mind that this is how we talk. It's way, way easier than actually talking about real stuff. And when I think about it, I don't want to talk about anything anyway, so having the Top 5 is a great crutch.

Sometimes between the pauses and the constant fidgeting with the radio—when I desperately try to keep him from listening to news or a song that he half knows and will try to sing to—I look at my dad and wonder if he's also glad we have the Top 5.

Maybe he's as foggy as I am and maybe it makes him less worried to simply ask me questions—the same questions over and over so he doesn't ever have to ask me any of the new ones, like *Are you okay?* and *How can I make us feel better?*

Secretly I think I want to be asked something real, and even though I don't have any answers, it's the questions I wish I could hear just so I'd know someone was thinking those things.

But the radio station starts playing a song he sort of knows, and then he's singing and the car is pulling up to the school, and I just let the fog take over and say, "See ya" and get out of the car reminding myself why tomorrow I am definitely just having toast for breakfast.

The door closes, and I'm about to walk off into the flow of kids with great names when I hear the car horn honk. I turn and see he hasn't driven off. The window near me is rolling down, and then my dad is leaning across the passenger's seat toward me.

"I forgot to tell you," he calls out loud enough for anyone to hear, but no one does even though it's being yelled at me. "We have a meeting with your math teacher after school."

And then the window goes up and he drives off, and I hate Mr. Shivnesky's head more than ever, and not even walking past Summer Goodman's locker three times while I pretend to look for a piece of paper makes me feel better.

If you've ever needed extra help in a school subject, then you know what I mean when I shout, "I HATE SCHOOL!"

Of course, I don't really shout it; in fact, when it comes to school, I barely even talk much. I once counted how many words I said aloud in one school day (bus ride not included) and that number was pretty low: 426. You should really try that some day and see just exactly how many words you let everyone else hear in one day.

The people I like to talk to are Marshall (duh)

and Mrs. Favius, my English teacher, who really knows her stuff. I am not one of those "honor roll" kids whose hand is always in the air and knows the answers without even hearing the full question. I bet if the honor students counted how many words they say every day, it would be in the millions because they raise their hands just to hear the sound of their own voices!

My day inches forward toward my after-school appointment with . . . MATH.

When I get to the doorway of Mr. Shivnesky's classroom at 3:35, my dad is already inside, and I can tell they were talking about me because they both instantly stop talking and smile and straighten up in their chairs.

"Milo," Mr. Shivnesky says, his smile as shiny as his head, which from the looks of it has just been waxed. "Look who's here." And that's just a dumb thing to say because of course I knew my dad was coming, but maybe he's just trying to cover up the fact that they were both just talking bad stuff about me and that I'm in big trouble, and I just want to shrink up and go home.

The next thirty minutes are a blur of me mostly not listening but nodding a lot. Adults really like it when you nod. I think it makes them feel like you're paying attention even when all you're really doing is counting from one to one hundred forward and then backward as many times as it takes just to get through this.

"So it's settled," Mr. Shivnesky says somewhere around my secretly thinking the number 72 for the eighth time. "Two days a week after school. Milo and I are going to crack this puppy."

Crack this puppy? And then I realize what he's said: *Two days after school?* With him? With *math*?

And then my dad and I are walking down the empty hallway together, and I can feel all those lockers watching me and it kind of feels weird to be in school with my dad, who as usual doesn't know what to say except, "That went well." Which is so what it wasn't that it makes me want to scream. But I don't.

And then Mr. Shivnesky shouts something down the hallway, and it stays with me a long time even after we get in the car and stop by the Chicken Cluck to buy take-home dinner. Mr. Shivnesky, the bald-headed evil genius, says, "Don't worry. Once you get past the confusing part, math makes sense."

Yeah, right.

pumpkin goop

I KNOW IT'S OCTOBER BECAUSE THE PIT STOP has a new Freezie flavor called "Booger Breath," which is neon orange and tastes like something you use to clean up the mess you just made from spitting out the stuff because it tastes so bad.

Pete says the Pit Stop always has a Halloween flavor that is supposed to gross you out but usually just makes kids feel like puking. Last year's Freezie was called "Gore 'N' Guts" and according to Pete, it was the exact same drink as Booger Breath except they made it green instead of orange, which to me sounds like it would taste better because mint chocolate chip ice cream tastes great but orange sherbet is the pits.

I like October, first of all, because it means September has finally bit the dust and, second, because the air starts to get cool enough to wear my hooded sweatshirts, which I love because of the fact that they make me feel invisible, like a superpower that goes in effect as soon as I close out the world by popping the hood over my head. If I were a real superhero, invisibility would definitely be my power, even though Marshall says being invisible would so lose out to practically any of the superpowers he'd have.

"Being invisible is a wimpy power." (Marshall says.)

"Oh, really? Well, you can't see me, so you don't know I am laughing in your face!" (I say.)

"Laser vision. Teleportation. Shape-shifting.

Those are *real* superpowers." (That's Marshall, and his list always changes, but you get the point.)

"Ha! I can listen to whatever people are saying about me and they don't even know I'm there." (And I pull the hood a little tighter.)

This is how it goes for most of the ride on the days I wear a hooded sweatshirt, which is a lot lately, so it's a conversation we're having a few days a week. And that's exactly what I like about having a friend like Marshall. You can talk about the same stuff over and over, like watching your favorite *Simpsons* episode, and it still feels fun.

"Even right now—you can't see me." (I say, making a weird face at him.)

"But I can smell you." (And this is his favorite line.)

Then we laugh, just as the bus pulls up to my stop.

I get off the bus two houses from where my house is. That's when I notice that the old lady across the street, the one who yells stuff at me that I never listen to, has already bought and carved a pumpkin. It's sitting on her top step like some sort of advertisement of what *not* to do because everyone knows only an idiot would go ahead and *carve a pumpkin* three and a half weeks before Halloween.

The fact that she did this shows how little she knows about things, and I think even less of her than I did before, which wasn't much mainly because she's always watching me from her living room window and waving at me, which can only mean she should get a cat.

There are two main rules when it comes to pumpkins, and the second is more important than the first but the first one matters too. Rule #1 is pretty simple: Pumpkins should only be bought in October.

There's no law that says you *can't* buy a September pumpkin, it's just that October is the month when you're supposed to do it—that's what my mother always told me every year when I'd beg and beg to get the first one I'd see at the fruit stand, which would usually be the first week of September. And even though the pumpkins were scrawny and looked like the puppy we once found who was so skinny that you could see his ribs and had patches of fur falling out all over, she'd explain the October rule of pumpkins to me and then let me buy it anyway because rules can be broken, especially when it's just a lopsided pumpkin. And we kept the puppy and named him Patches.

Rule #2 is the big deal breaker, and if you

disobey that rule, then you must just be goofy in the head, which might explain a lot about you-know-who across the street, who sometimes goes outside to get her newspaper wearing a bathrobe and big green rubber boots.

Pumpkin Rule #2 insists that you don't carve your pumpkin until *exactly one week* before Halloween—the same day you scoop out all the guts with your hands and hold up the drippy slime and threaten to wash your sister's hair with it until she screams at you and you just do it anyway.

That's when you clean the guck off the seeds and then you and your mom spread them out on the salted cookie sheet and bake them, and even though the whole house smells good, you really don't like how they taste, but you eat them anyway because it's a week before Halloween and everyone's in the kitchen laughing.

That's the day when you carve the pumpkins, and you have four of them—one for everybody—and even your sister has fun carving out the fat chunks and making the faces look as scary as you can.

But the lady across the street obviously doesn't know this, and by breaking Rule #2, she'll find out the hard way that by the time Halloween rolls around, the squirrels will have eaten half her pumpkin or it will have already started to rot, which makes the face droop.

Last year was the second October after the fog settled in but the first time I didn't carve a pumpkin.

No matter how hard my dad begged me to do it, and he even spread out newspaper on the kitchen table and preheated the oven and told me it would be "good" for me, I told him no and just ended up sneaking outside after he'd gone to bed and smashing the pumpkin on the driveway even though I knew he'd done the right thing and bought it in October.

The next morning I kept waiting for him to talk to me about the busted pumpkin, but he never said a word, and by the time I came home from school, the mess had already been cleaned up like nothing had ever happened, which is pretty much business as usual around my house.

Up in my room I "get organized," which means I lift up my backpack and turn it upside down so that all the books and papers and half-eaten things spill out and make even more of a mess of my unmade bed.

- Gum wrapper with chewed gum inside, which represents the "warning" I get in study hall for breaking the No Gum Chewing law

- Stinky balled-up gym shirt, which reminds me not to sweat so much—it's just gross
- Half of Marshall's peanut-butter-and-marshmallow sandwich, which I couldn't eat during science, where Mr. Gnit would never know because he doesn't ever look at us, but we had a substitute with actual VISION so now I have to scrape peanut butter and marshmallow off my books

And then I see the folded piece of purple paper lying under my grammar book and I know instantly it came from Hillary Alpert, and even if I didn't instantly know it, the words *From the desk of Hillary Alpert* at the top of the page would certainly clue me in. I bet the notepaper was a birthday present from her grandma, who had pads and pads of the stuff made for her, which sounds nice but gimme a break—who wants paper with your name on it for a present? Oh, right. Hillary would!

Anyway, Hillary Alpert has been shoving these purple notes into my locker every couple of days, and I pretty much stopped reading them after I figured out they didn't *mean* anything. I mean, if Hillary was asking me for the answers to the geography quiz, I could do that. If she wanted to find out if I had any gum, I could lie and tell her no. But her notes mostly just say things like, *Hi* and *What's up?* and *Hope you have a super Friday*, and I don't know how to answer those kind of notes—so I just crumple them up and chuck them in the trash.

My sister keeps telling me Hillary's notes are a "sign," and when I look at her with my eyebrows squished, she laughs and says, "She likes you, doofus!" I explain how ridiculous that is because Hillary Alpert is weird and eats lunch at a different table every day and that it would be impossible to like her anyway—because I have already committed myself to someone else (I don't say the name "Summer Goodman" on the grounds that my sister might use it against me).

But my sister tells me, as if she's the expert: "Look, you can't let a girl think it's okay to like you if you don't like her back. Trust me. Tell this girl you aren't interested. It's the right thing to do, Milo."

That's why I'm standing there crumpling that purple paper into a ball. If I want to put a stop to the note invasion and, according to my sister, "do the right thing," I have to have a "Real Talk" with Hillary Alpert.

Fine, I tell myself. *Done deal!*

Then, for the reason that I really don't want to start my homework, I do something I never do. Instead of making believe I'm a professional basketball player and using Hillary's note to sink a basket with three seconds left on the clock, I uncrumple the purple ball. Maybe I am curious about what kind of dumb thing she wants to tell me this time, or maybe I hope there's a ten-dollar bill taped inside the purple page. Whatever the reason, it doesn't matter because as soon as I see what she's written, I don't even mind looking at all of her curly-girly handwriting with the dopey smiley faces that dot her *i*'s and j's.

She wrote:

r.s.v.p. r.i.p.

I'M IN A PICKLE.

Literally.

I'm inside a costume and it's shaped like a pickle and I have to go to the bathroom but there's no one to help me see where I'm going, and because the eye slits are about two inches above my eyes, I just keep bouncing off of things like a pinball and I know I am in trouble and there's no zipper that I can find on the dumb thing, and all I can think about is:

Why did I think a pickle would be a good costume?

I wake up and breathe that sigh of relief that comes when you realize the terrible thing you just thought was real is really just a dream, and I am not in a pickle costume but in my bed and the clock says 6:52, which means I still have eight minutes to lie here before the alarm goes off and my dad pokes his head in the door and says, "Get up, Milo, and I mean it, right now, mister."

I have to use those eight minutes wisely, and it takes me two of those minutes to figure out how to best use the leftover six, which is to carefully weigh out the pros and cons of my current life situation.

Here's what I need to consider: Do I break up with Hillary Alpert right away or wait until after Summer Goodman's party?

It takes me about three and a half of my stay-in-bed minutes to realize that the answer is a no-brainer and that there's no reason to rush into the mess of hurting Hillary's feelings when I have more immediate things to think about, by which I mean: making sure everything is in place for me to go to Summer's Halloween party.

I start making a list of ten great costumes I could be, but before I even get past the first two—(1) a human calculator and (2) Mr. Potato Head's cousin, "Señor Squash"—the alarm goes off, my dad's head pokes in, and my day is no longer mine.

And then, like dominoes, it all goes like this:

- Shower
- Breakfast (not Cheerios so I take the bus)
- School (no tests, just a pop quiz in English, which I ace because I rock!)
- Math (I want to make it illegal to use numbers in any way except to rate a movie)

Finally, school is out—but because I go to Mr. Shivnesky's classroom two days a week from 3:30 to 4:15, that's where I end up. And it's like torture because it's just him and me and I can't pretend I'm listening but am really drawing in my notebook; I have to pay *actual* attention because he's right in front of me all the time, and the worst part is that when he talks, all I see is that big smooth head that sometimes has nubs and sometimes doesn't. It's weird. Today I see that his head is extra shiny and smells funny, and I worry he is using salad dressing on his scalp because his head-stink reminds me of going to an Italian restaurant. I am just about to ask him if he likes garlic bread sticks when he says, "Milo, you're not concentrating." And I realize that he says this exact thing to me so often that it should become his catchphrase and I want to get him a T-shirt that says, MILO, YOU'RE NOT CONCENTRATING. That, or find him a job on a sitcom where every week that's the only thing he says and everyone in the audience would laugh.

"Milo . . ."

I know. I'm not concentrating, and he presents the problem to me again.

I try to explain that my brain doesn't work the way he wants, but he just smiles and asks me to try again and he's so calm about it, I want to scream.

Finally, it's 4:15 and I get to ditch Egghead and catch up with Marshall at the Pit Stop. We have decided to make it our life goal to somehow try to stomach a whole Booger Breath Freezie before Halloween. It's not a pretty sight (or smell) but we're determined to do it because then we'd have something to brag about—but once again the taste is so much like boiled socks that we still only manage to drink half.

"What if we ask Pete to skip the booger part?" Marshall suggests, but we both know that would be cheating, so we each take another sip before tossing the half-full stinky cups into the trash and rinsing the flavor out of our mouths by buying a quart of chocolate milk and passing it back and forth until it's totally all gone.

"Marshall," I say as I wipe my chocolate mustache onto my sleeve, "I have some serious news." And he knows I mean business, so he crosses his arms and listens real close. I tell Marshall about Summer Goodman's Halloween party, and even before I get to the part where we start to brainstorm cool ways we could go as cyborg clones or human-size game pieces from Monopoly, he points out the obvious downfall of the whole plan:

Poor Marshall. He doesn't know that *I know* my invitation is in the mail—either that or it's been stuffed by accident in a drawer somewhere or was left inside the wrong mailbox but is definitely on its way to my house, probably even while I stand there feeling sick inside.

"Milo," Marshall says, and I can't figure out why he isn't excited. But his words just stop like he ran out of them, and he chews on the inside of his cheeks in the way that tells me he's thinking of something. Then the next thing is, he agrees he'll go to Summer's party even though he is positive it is way out of our league.

I ask him what that means, but One-Eyed Jack just shrugs and says, "We're doomed."

That night I spend two hours going through the recycle bin in the garage just in case my sister thought she was saving a tree by putting my Halloween invitation in the pile, but all I come up with is a paper cut and two coupons for meatball subs at the Pit Stop, which I will definitely use but only after they stop serving those disgusting Freezies.

In between my ten-minute breaks, which I schedule every fifteen minutes, I think about what Marshall said about Summer's party being "out of our league" and decide there are two kinds of kids when it comes to going to parties:

First there are the "Hey, I love going to somebody else's house and hanging around with kids I see every day, eating potato chips and laughing at funny jokes" kind of kids. These are most of the kids you see every day in school who just know their whole lives are great and they never have to check to see if there's toilet paper stuck to their shoe.

Then there's the second kind. These are the "Why would I want to go to a party with the same kids who point at me because I have toilet paper stuck to my shoe?" kind of kids.

And then I get it. Marshall thinks we're the

second kind—but he forgets it's Halloween, which means you wear a costume and can pretend you're the first kind, and since everyone is in a costume pretending to be someone else, it's an even score right from the start, which really only comes once a year and that day is this Friday and I can't wait. And I can't find my invitation either.

The next day is Wednesday, so it's an excellent day already because I don't have to see Mr. Shivnesky's head after school and it gets even better because right away, before I even undo my locker combination, I see Summer walking right toward me. She's with Felicia (who they say is really nice) and Darcy (who isn't), and the three of them fill the hallway with the sound of clicking shoes and the smell of strawberry gum.

Because they're so busy talking and laughing, I get to stare extra long at Summer, which I do from behind my geography book, and I imagine she is laughing and talking about me and how she can't wait to see the fantastic costume I come up with for her party.

"Just you wait, Summer," I by accident say OUT LOUD, and I say it just as she passes me, and all of a sudden my heart goes nuts because she stops and looks right at me.

"What?" Summer Goodman says, and she is actually saying this to me. And all three of them are staring at me and I can't believe it, so I try to look extra supercool and lean against my locker, which unfortunately is about a foot farther away than I thought, and the next thing I know, I am on the floor and she's laughing and it's a beautiful laugh even if it does make my face really red.

Dabney St. Claire whispers in my ear, *Stay cool. You meant to do that.* So I strike a casual pose, as if falling on the floor is the most natural thing to do ever, which for me it kind of is.

Before I can say anything, Darcy tugs on Summer and then all three click-clack off, and it's just the smell of the gum and my red face that's left behind, but that's still enough to remind me that Summer Goodman spoke to me today, which makes it a memory even if my butt bone still hurts.

Spanish class. Señora McCarthy is busy reviewing verbs, which gives me time to work on my Halloween costume list, which I try to do *en español* just to be fair:

Pickle Hat

- una hamburguesa

- el Godzilla

- lápiz gigante

When Señora McCarthy walks past my desk, she isn't as impressed as I think she should be because even if I wasn't paying attention, I *was* doing it in Spanish, so I think having to do extra homework is *muy, muy* unfair.

That night I check our mailbox three times. And then I go up and down the street checking other mailboxes just in case, which was a waste of time and I hate barking dogs.

Thursday. I tell Marshall a lie just so he can relax and not break out in hives, which WebMD says is a nervous disorder that can be painful.

"Yup. The invite came in the mail yesterday." This is my lie, and I say it so loud that even Hillary Alpert hears me and then later I find a purple note in my locker. At first I am afraid it is yet another love note, but in truth all it says is: *Heard you're going to the party. Do you guys want a ride?*

Even though I know I have to break things off

with her, when I see her in the hallway, I casually tell Hillary, "Sure, catching a ride to the party would be great." Then I tell her she better watch out when she sees my costume, and when she asks what my costume is, I realize I don't know and then it hits me that I've been too busy searching for the missing invitation and making lists of great costume ideas that I haven't actually *made* a costume yet and a tiny panic sets inside my stomach.

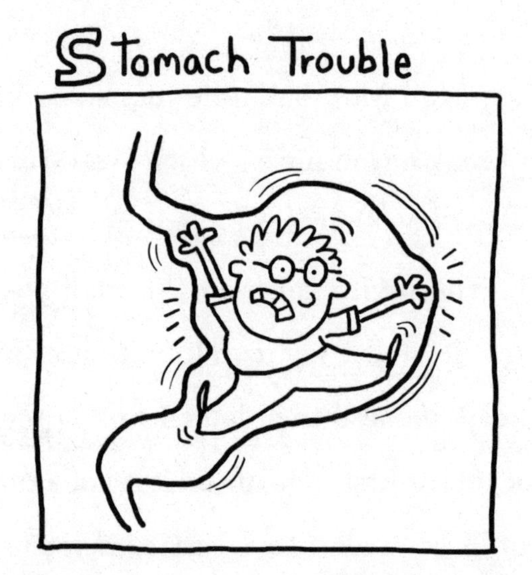

"My costume is a secret," is what I say, but what I think is: *I am starting to break out in hives.*

jell-o brains

THE BIG NIGHT ARRIVES, AND I'M STILL mad at my dad because I'm sure he's the one who threw my invitation away just so my whole life could be ruined. And I'm mad at my sister because she didn't stop my dad from ruining my life. And I'm mad at my mom for not being here to make me a costume at the last minute like she always used to do when I was a kid.

At 6:15 Marshall comes over, and he's a scare-crow. I give him an A for effort, mainly because of the real straw pieces coming out of his shirt and the plastic crow his mom sewed on to his shoulder, even if it keeps drooping over like it's dead.

"Cool costume," I say.

"I'm itchy," he says back. "Real, real itchy."

And then he takes a piece of straw out of his shirt and uses it to try to reach around his back for a scratchy spot, and I envy him because at least he has a costume and I'm just standing there in my normal clothes.

And that's when I break the news to him. "Marshall, I kind of lied," I say. "I can't find my invitation. I don't think we can go."

My pal, One-Eyed Jack the Scarecrow, doesn't

bat an eye, though he does keep scratching himself all over. "Oh. No sweat," he says, and I think he's smiling. And no sooner is he pulling handfuls of itchy straw out of his flannel shirt than the doorbell rings, and my heart soars because it has to be a special delivery mailman who is here to apologize about my Halloween party invitation being found stuck to the bottom of the mailman's bag, and they really should be more careful about these things and I hope he got a post office detention.

The bell rings again and I open the door, but it isn't the mailman—it's some crazy gypsy who has a wart on her nose and two gold teeth. So I just close the door fast.

"Milo!" the gypsy screams, and then I think, *Oh no, she's somehow read into my mind!* So I open the door and see the gypsy is really Hillary.

"Come on. My dad's waiting," Hillary the Gypsy says.

"Sorry. We can't go," Marshall tells her. "Milo can't find the invite." And he says this not in a way that sounds disappointed, more like he just said, *Let's all watch* Zombie Bats II *on cable!*

Hillary looks at Marshall, who still scratches all over like crazy, and then at me, who's not even in a costume, and says, "You don't need an invitation if you walk in with me."

Marshall says, "Well, actually—"

And I jump in and finish his sentence by saying, "That sounds great!"

And the next thing I know, I'm up in my room grabbing anything I can find to make an instant costume, and I think I do pretty good too, even if Hillary's dad keeps looking at me weird in the car's rearview mirror.

Summer Goodman's house is all lit up outside with orange lights and blinking ghosts. There are six perfectly carved pumpkins lining the walk to the

front door, and only one of them has a face that has started to rot—so I know they follow the pumpkin rules pretty closely. We get out of the car and say "thanks" and then follow the line of kids in costumes toward the front door of Summer's house.

Standing in the middle of goblins and devils and witches and the one kid who is a refrigerator, I realize I don't recognize a single person, so I immediately feel like a million bucks.

"I dunno about this," Marshall says, looking at all the kids waiting to get inside.

We follow Dracula and two cowgirls, who clearly showed up in the same store-bought costume and are not happy about it. The line to get into the house moves slowly, which I finally see is because there's a princess at the front door and the princess is Summer and she's being pretty and making sure no one tries to sneak in.

We're finally next to get in. I can hear cool music and can see into the house, where it looks like a real live party, the kind kids on TV go to, and there are cobwebs and dangling spiders and tons of kids wearing scary stuff, or silly stuff, or in the case of Mark Tompkins, just a fedora-type hat and a black turtleneck, which is just totally lame.

And then the line moves forward, and there we are—over the threshold and in the presence of the princess. I smell hot cider and popcorn and am standing next to Summer, who looks incredible, even though I'm pretty sure it's a costume that you rent, which is one step better than one that you buy, but nowhere near as good as a homemade one.

"Hi, Summer," Hillary the Gypsy says, and Marshall is busy scratching, and I stand there and let my costume speak for itself even though I've already lost one of my sock tentacles.

"Hillary!" Summer says. "Thanks so much for coming."

Did you hear that? Dabney St. Claire whispers to me. *She thanked you for coming.* In my mind I tell Dabney St. Claire that she actually thanked *Hillary* for coming, and then he tells me to just "go with it," and the next thing I hear is Hillary saying . . .

"Summer, this is Marshall and Milo. They came with me."

I watch as Summer's princess face scrunches up like she just got asked, *What is the square root of 756?* And then Summer says, "Oh, I don't think I know them. . . . But have a good time!"

And even though we're now officially inside the party, I suddenly feel like maybe being home would be a better place to be. But then I realize I'm sure it was my costume that got in the way of Summer knowing me, and then I wish I'd used the costume that Mark Tompkins used, which is no costume at all.

"Milo, the mini hot dogs are wicked!" Marshall seems to figure out that eating stops the itchiness, so he has made a sport out of trying all the stuff that's in bowls or on trays and is giving me a play-by-play. "And you gotta try these eyeball brownies. Man, I am so glad you made me come!"

I look over the table full of foodstuff, most of which is made to look creepy. I see pretzel sticks dipped in red frosting with a sign that says BLOODY FINGERS, and I see the brownies that Marshall is now eating two at a time decorated with eyeballs on top. There are ghost cookies and a pumpkin-shaped cake, and my stomach is so flip-floppy that I settle for a cup of cider and try to look like this is fun.

Hillary is off with some girls I don't know, and I'm shocked she has friends because I never pictured that

or saw her at school hanging around with anyone.

See that? Dabney St. Claire whispers to me, and I have to ask him to speak up because the music got even louder. *She's making conversation. That's what you do at parties.*

I never thought of conversation as something you have to "make," which maybe explains why it's so hard for me to actually talk out loud. Still, I decide to take Dabney St. Claire's advice, and I wander to the part of the party that seems the quietest and turn to a kid who is dressed as a huge red tomato, who I recognize as a girl who I think is in my Spanish class.

She is standing by herself too, so I figure this might just work out great.

"Hola," I say using all of my Spanish skills at once. *"Me llamo Milo."*

Dabney St. Claire gives me a thumbs-up, which is way better than what the tomato gives me—a look like I am the thing she just stepped in that smells bad.

A second later the tomato is gone, and I am watching the party like it is on TV at home, only I can't change the channel or even turn it off.

The kitchen door is open so I walk inside, and a lady who is either Summer's mom or a very pretty teacher is filling cups with a punchlike drink that unfortunately has the same look and color of Booger Breath Freezies.

"Oh, hello," the lady says once she sees me standing next to her. "Are you lost?"

"Nope." And it's true because any fool would know this is the kitchen.

She seems really nice but doesn't talk to me.

After a few seconds of this silent stuff she wipes her hands on her skeleton apron and looks at me like she's trying to guess my weight or think what is my favorite color (green!).

"Hey, have you been to the haunted house yet?" she decides to say to me. "It's in the basement. It's really fun!"

"Cool," I say, and I let her lead me out of the kitchen and point me to a door with a skeleton on it and words that say ENTER AT YOUR OWN RISK, and I ask her if I need to sign a waiver, which is what people do before doing dangerous stuff like skydiving.

The next thing I know, I am walking down a dim staircase and cobwebs touch my face and the sounds of scary music and screams are everywhere. At the bottom of the stairs is a hose or something that puffs a blast of air right at you, and it scares me because it's such a surprise.

I am just about to turn around and go back, but the door opens at the top of the stairs and now more kids are coming down, and I decide it's probably better to just move forward and get this over with.

First there's a bowl of eyeballs you have to touch, and even though I know they're just skinless grapes, it still is pretty gross.

Next a kid who I bet is Summer's older brother

jumps out of a dark corner waving a fake bloody arm at me, which I admit is scary, not because of the arm, but because of the jumping-out-of-the-corner part.

There are bright green arrows that point the way, and the haunted house leads on into a small room filled with Day-Glo lightbulbs that make all the white cobwebs glow like they're radioactive and so do my sneakers and so do the skeletons that drop down from the ceiling. I like this part because my white socks seem to be alive, and I would just hang out here if a kid didn't shout, "Keep the line moving!" So I walk out of the Day-Glo room and into a pitch-black place.

Now, I'm not a fan of dark places, but Dabney St. Claire tells me to breathe and so I do, and after a second or two of dark silence where I can only hear some of the music from the party upstairs, a creepy voice from a loudspeaker in the ceiling says, "It's time to meet Bloody Mary."

Then there's a scream (and it isn't me).

Then a spotlight turns on, and there's a teenager standing in front of me covered in blood and her head is cut open and she holds her own brain in her hands.

And then there's another scream, and this one *is* from me.

Bloody Mary takes a step toward me and says, "Touch my brain," and she pushes the gooey red thing right at me and I am frozen stiff and I can't breathe too good, and I must look scared because Bloody Mary laughs and takes my hand and sticks it right into her brain!

And even though I know it's all fake and the brain is just Jell-O, I am already running. And I don't know how to get out of the basement or how to get away from the party, but I have to. I have to get away. Help me get away!

And then all the basement lights go on, which erases the haunted house, and I hear kids say,

"Awwww, man." And the lady with the skeleton on her apron is taking me outside through the back basement door. And the stars are so bright and the air so cold that I finally breathe again, and I'm sure I'm not crying but she gives me a tissue anyway. And driving home in the backseat of my dad's car, on account of he had to be called to come and get me, I don't talk about anything. And he doesn't ask.

tiny breaths

THE HALLOWEEN PARTY INCIDENT GETS wiped clean as soon as October comes to an end, which thankfully happens really fast. By Monday it's November, and I'm relieved that Summer has the decency not to ask what happened in her basement. In fact, each time I see her, she stays silent, which makes me feel like we are both sharing the same secret, though I'm not sure which one it is.

November is great because the days start off chilly, which is something I like because it's cold enough to see your breath, but only for an hour or so before the sun warms things up.

When I was really little, I asked my mom why smoke came out of my mouth in the winter. First she smiled. Then she used her mitten to rub the snot from my drippy nose, which just made it all itchy. She told me it wasn't smoke. She said that letting our breath out is how we make wishes come true and that winter is the best time for wishing because when it's cold, we actually get to see each wish come out and drift away in the sky.

Of course, I'm not little anymore, and I know the real reason why I can see my breath has to do with moisture and CO_2 and the cold temperature outside. But that doesn't stop me from imagining that every time I breathe out, I get my wish as I count the seconds it takes for her to drift away from me again.

the museum of busted stuff

THE PURPLE NOTE IN MY LOCKER SAYS, MY HOUSE AFTER SCHOOL. WANT TO?

And so with my sister's advice about breakups in my head . . .

. . . I make the journey from the steps of my house, down ten feet of sidewalk, and up the walk to Hillary's front door.

The door opens before I can even find the doorbell, which I wasn't sure I was going to actually ring. "Milo! Fantastic!" And with those words, I know there is no turning back.

Hillary's house is much neater than mine, which isn't saying a lot, seeing as my house looks like a tornado lives there. All those clean surfaces make me a little nervous, but since I've never been inside before, I let her show me around like it's a museum and she's the tour guide:

"This is the piano where I take my lessons."

"Over here is my mom's favorite plant that you can't kill no matter how much you water it."

"My dad likes this chair because it leans backward."

She shows me the kitchen and asks if I want some fruit. I say no, fighting hard the feeling that tugs at me and says, *Go home!* because I hate that I am here to break the BIG NEWS about our doomed relationship. Maybe she senses I want to run, which is probably why she opens a bag of chocolate chip cookies and offers me as many as I want, which is three.

I see pictures on the refrigerator and everyone is laughing and there's no one missing, which reminds me that we don't hang anything on our fridge anymore except emergency phone numbers.

"Look, Hillary," I say, and my stomach wants to explode. I have to tell her the truth about how I don't like her.

She stops what she's doing (cutting an apple into ten identical slices), and I can tell I have her attention.

Most kids would look away after someone who started talking didn't keep talking, but Hillary is different, so she just keeps looking at me with her head tilted to the side. And I don't say anything and feel awful.

"Do you want to see my room?" She takes charge again and decides to move things along, and I am actually so glad the tour has restarted that I nod my head yes and then take two more cookies just in case she decides to show me the attic and basement too.

Walking down the hallway lined with Hillary's family photographs, I realize there's a smell in her house, and as soon as I put a finger on it, I really miss it. It's lemon Pledge, which comes in a can and makes things shiny, and it's one of those smells that belongs to my mom and it actually makes me feel happy not sad to smell it again—though I am slightly embarrassed Hillary catches me sniffing things.

Hillary's bedroom door has a brass nameplate on it like those doors to an office where somebody works. HILLARY R. ALPERT it says, and before she opens the door for me, she stands next to it and smiles like she's proud that her door has the same name that she does.

"The 'R' stands for Rebecca," she tells me, and I nod like now I know all the secrets of the world.

Inside it really looks like a museum, like one of those roped-off rooms where they don't let people inside. First off, her bed looks like there's no way it's ever been slept on, and there isn't one piece of clothing on the floor. Looking around, I see that the desk is arranged like an ad on TV, and the room smells nice—but not girly nice, just nice in the lemon Pledge sort of way.

"Sit anywhere," Hillary says, which I'm kind of afraid to do, seeing as the bed is like a frosted cake and I don't want to be the one to ruin it with my butt.

While I try to find a sitting-down spot that will cause her room the least disruption, she opens her closet and I see the reason her room is so perfect: Her closet looks like her room threw up in it. Stuff is everywhere—clothes, books, some old toys and games that I bet she hasn't played with for forever.

And I smile for the first time since I got to her house.

I finally decide that the floor is the safest bet, so I sit down and get ready to have my "talk," and inside I feel lousy even though on the outside I look fine.

"Are you okay?" Hillary is staring at me. "You look awful."

"It's like this," I say. "I want you to know I think you're really nice." (This is a lie because I don't think she's really nice—I think she's kind of a pain; but my sister says that telling the total truth is the wrong way to go in a breakup.)

"I think you're nice too." She isn't looking at me anymore—she's reaching for something under her bed. And for the brief second when she lifts her bedspread, I see that under her bed is like a junkyard of boxes and massive dust balls, and to be honest, I sort of start to like her a little.

"The thing is," I continue, knowing that if I don't say what I have to say, those purple notes are going to be the death of me. "I know you like me and—"

I can't even finish my sentence because Hillary Rebecca Alpert is laughing and my face heats up and I know I just made a jerk out of myself.

"Milo, of course I like you." Now she stops laughing mainly because I think she sees my own face, which is probably one of terror. "But you think I like you—you know, in a boyfriend-slash-crush kind of way?"

I know I should deny it and answer the other way, but instead I say, "Well, yeah." And my face doesn't feel so red, but I do feel like an idiot. "All those notes . . . and phone calls . . ."

"That's called being nice," Hillary says. "I'm way not ready to like a boy. Not like *that,* anyway."

My fingers are crisscrossed real tight, like I'm

praying, but I'm not. I'm just really uncomfortable. But then Hillary does something amazing. She just moves on, kind of like we'd just been talking about turtles or something and not what a bonehead I was. "Want to see something kind of weird?"

And of course I say yes. Anything to get away from the moment works for me, and that's when she shows me the box she's holding in her lap. It's just a beat-up shoe box and it's pretty old, which I can see from the tape that holds the corners together and some of the writing on the sides, which is in crayon.

"You won't laugh? Promise, okay?"

And because I was just such a doofus, this is the easiest promise I've ever made, and then she slowly lifts off the shoe box top and shows me what's inside.

"Creepy, isn't it?" Hillary asks as I stare into a mangled mess of plastic doll heads and discarded body parts. "I've been collecting them forever."

I am kind of fascinated by this new thing. Right before my eyes, stuck-up Hillary with her perfect

purple notes is turning into a cool person, the kind I might not hang up on the next time she calls to ask if I want to watch TV.

"I dunno why," she says, lifting up half of a doll that at one point in time was a whole Barbie but now is just a mess. "I've always collected the broken dolls. The ones no one wants anymore." She twists the torso, and the head of the doll formerly known as Barbie pops off and rolls to my foot. "When I was a kid, I'd make my mom take me to yard sales so I could find the leftover broken pieces. Every weekend. For hours. I was obsessed!"

Hillary dips her hand into the sea of plastic

like she's fishing for a busted leg or maybe a three-fingered hand. "I know. Total weirdo stuff, right?"

Even though I think it's a little strange, I say, "No way. It's cool." And then I reach into the box and rummage around and imagine all the dolls that had to die to fill the box. I picture doll family funerals and the sad dollhouses where now a doll dad has to deal with his doll kids and the doll mom who isn't coming home.

I tell Hillary this, thinking it will make her think I think her shoe box is a superneat thing, but her reaction isn't at all what I was hoping for.

"Milo." Her voice is softer than before and there's a pause, so I wonder what's about to follow. "What was it like . . . you know, with your mom?"

I'm staring into the box of arms and heads and crooked little legs when I hear the words, and when I look back up, her head is tilted again and she reminds me of Patches when he wants to decide whether he's going to pee outside or on the couch.

At first I can't believe she's asked me this—and I really want to get up and run out of her house, slamming each door along the way as hard as I can. But then it's okay because I realize she really wants to know. . . . And I don't know why I do it. Maybe it's the five cookies she gave me or maybe it's because I feel bad that I thought she liked me and I didn't like her, but now that she doesn't, I kind of do.

Either way, that's when I start to talk.

It all happened so fast, I say, and because you're not paying attention, it's over before you can even catch on that something huge has just changed everything you ever knew. I tell her it's like in a movie when they erase some guy's memory, only they don't do a good job and he sort of remembers stuff but only kind of. I tell her that's what the fog is. I stop talking and think Hillary is going to ask me something, but she's just watching me and I can tell that if I go on or if I stop, she's not going to care. To be honest, I'm not sure if I'm done or not, but I take a breath and before I know it, more words are coming out of my mouth.

I tell Hillary: First came the headaches. Then the afternoon naps. Then she and my dad did a lot of whispering and her smile was always there, like she knew she had to make sure it was what we'd always remember—but what I remember most is that I used to feel different inside.

Hillary asks if I want to stop. Maybe she sees that I'm shaking just a little bit or maybe deep down she's a person who is actually really nice and not a brat. But I don't want to stop, I want to keep talking, so I look down at the rug I'm sitting on and follow the swirly patterns with my eyes like it's a maze I have to navigate. And then I close my eyes and start talking again. . . .

To tell the whole story, I have to reach through the fog and push it all aside so I can see again. And it feels bad to think so hard about it all—but no one ever talks about this and there's a little part of me that wants to listen to the story, so I dig down deep and try. I realize it's kind of like flying, and in my head I'm going back in time, soaring toward the Fog House, and then I see my old street and there's Steven Siegel and he's playing basketball in his driveway and he's cheating the way he always did by double dribbling *and* traveling, and then I see my house and I fly inside and I see us—my family—and I just watch it all happen the way it did and it's as if I'm a ghost watching them, which is kind of creepy but I don't care.

There we all are sitting on the blue couch, and we never sit on the blue couch because the blue couch is in the living room and we only sat there if it was a holiday, but that day was a Tuesday and holidays are usually on Mondays or Fridays.

My parents hold hands and my sister fidgets with her braces and sighs because she's bored and probably has a hundred things to do, which usually means she wants to go back to her dumb room and talk on the phone with her friends, but she sits there like I do, thinking we're about to discuss some family "thing," like whether we really should finally give Patches away or where we should go on vacation this summer and I pray it isn't camping again because I hated sleeping on the ground *and* I got poison ivy.

"Your mom is sick," my dad finally says, and at first I wonder what the fuss is about—we all get sick. In fact, I threw up just two weeks ago and had to eat chicken broth and crackers for two whole days, so I think, *So what?* Then I sneak a quick look at my mom and she's still smiling and she looks okay, so I really wonder if this is some sort of joke.

"What do you mean, 'sick'?" my sister asks, and because she's older, I think maybe she sees through the haze and can tell something real is happening even while I pretend it isn't.

Nobody answers, and suddenly I'm fidgeting too. "I want to go back to my show," I say, pleading to slink off to the den so I can watch *Wheel of Fortune* because I'm really good at guessing the words, especially when they are looking for a "phrase" or a "thing" but not a "person" because I never know who people like Liberace or Humphrey Bogart are.

My mother reaches for my shoulder and her touch makes me stay, and when I look up in her face, I see the hint of tears and then it hits me so hard that I freeze inside because SOMETHING IS WRONG.

"I need to go in the hospital," she says all calm. "Just a few tests and then we'll know more."

Know more? More about what? What do they need to know?

The phone rings, and then I realize I'm back in Hillary's room and I'm holding the top half of one of her rescue dolls in my hands and I'm squeezing it really hard. Hillary isn't sitting on her bed anymore. Somehow she's now on the floor with me and she's looking at me in a way that I just can't stand.

"I gotta go." And I do. I stand up and I can't look at her, and she says, "Okay," and I say, "Thanks for the cookies." And then I walk next door and go upstairs and sit on my bed and it isn't until supper that I realize I'm still clutching the broken doll piece in my fist.

Suddenly, the thing looks like a hand grenade, and the only thing I can do is try to blow up what just happened—so I open my window and twist off the head and throw both pieces into the darkness.

I lie back on my bed and count to five and then mouth the word that I hope will erase the last two hours.

"Boom."

brain scans

I DON'T KNOW WHAT SCIENCE-FICTION THINGS happen inside a brain to make the cells go crazy and change and then turn into cancer. I just know that when my head throbs or I get the slightest pain behind my eyes, I don't get an aspirin.

I get scared.

When your mother dies because of a tumor in her brain, it's pretty hard not to think that every time you get a headache, you've got one too. I know that sounds a little kooky, like yelling "Fire!" because someone lit a match, but my mom's headache was the first chapter in the story that was the end—so it's not such a huge leap to make.

equal signs

EQUATIONS ARE WHAT I'M HAVING SUCH a hard time with. That's why I stay after school two days a week. It's Monday so I have no choice but to drag my butt to Mr. Shivnesky's dumb room. The truth is, Mr. Shivnesky is really a pretty nice guy once you get past the whole head thing, and to do this, I picture different styles of haircuts that would make both our lives better:

I decide he's a good teacher, which doesn't mean I'm making much progress, but he doesn't get mad at me when I keep not getting it and he gives me a five-minute break whenever I need one—except when it's because I'm being lazy.

Five minutes isn't a ton of time, but it is enough to take a walk around the hallways, which is exactly what I decide to do. Walking past the French room, I hear a sound that makes my feet stop.

"I'm sorry," the voice says. "I can't use the past tense because I don't know the word." The voice is Summer's voice, and I instantly forget that I only have two minutes and forty-three seconds left on my break. Dabney St. Claire tells me that now's my chance to swoop in and save the day, but I have to remind him that I don't know French. I barely know Spanish.

Come on, Dabney St. Claire says. *Go say something to her. What's the worst that can happen?*

In my head I answer him by making this list:

The WORST that could happen

I am arrested for invading her "space."

Instead of **WORDS**, I speak in a language of SPIT SPRAY!

A meteor crashes to Earth and lands in the EXACT SPOT I am standing—just as I am ready to actually speak to her!

While I stand there stuck in time, time marches on.

Beep-beep. Beep-beep. Beep-beep. Beep-beep.

It's my watch alarm reminding me my break is over, and I have to abandon Summer and rush back to Mr. Shivnesky, who just opens the math book and picks up where we left off, which is me not understanding anything and him being patient.

Mr. Shivnesky asks me what I plan to do over the winter break. They can't call it "Christmas vacation" anymore mainly because everyone doesn't celebrate Christmas and some people got mad, which I guess makes sense, except for the fact that "winter break" sounds lame and not half as much fun. Truth is, I hate December almost as much as I hate September but not nearly as much as June.

Holidays are really hard in my house, and the whole Christmas–Hanukkah–New Year's stretch just lays there all flat and empty.

My sister caught on last year, and this year made her own plans to go away with Cynthia Boyd's family over "the holidays," which is fine by my dad, but the bad part is, then it's just me and him and way too much nothing to do.

I don't say any of this to Mr. Shivnesky. I lie and tell him that we like to go to the Bahamas over the holidays, which is something I heard Rachel Grenier tell Donna Rubin in the cafeteria.

Mr. Shivnesky says that sounds nice, and suddenly an equation pops into my head and it looks like this: ME = $x - y$ (x = US, y = HER).

a purple p.s.

Then I rip the note into a million pieces

and throw them into the trash can.

sleepover

THE ONLY PROBLEM WITH CALLING A vacation a "break" is that it reminds me that everything in my house actually does feel broken. Don't get me wrong. Ten days of not going to school makes me happier than Patches when he gets to scratch himself against the side of the couch (when even more fur falls off). It's just that hanging around with nothing much to do makes the house get quieter, and it just makes me remember how loud everything used to be.

But none of that really matters because I'm at Marshall's house and not just to hang out after school and not to use his computer to Google the traffic to see if my dad's going to have a safe ride home—I'm there for a sleepover, and I feel like I'm on the greatest vacation ever.

I'm lucky for the reason that Marshall's grandmother is a wild woman, which means he and his family didn't have to drive to Arizona over the "winter break" on account that she (his grandma) decided at the last minute to go on a singles cruise, where she plans to find a new boyfriend.

Now, I'm no relationship expert, but to me, once you're older than a certain age, I don't think you should still call people "boyfriend" and "girlfriend" anymore. I think that age is probably seventeen or maybe twenty. In my head it just feels spooky to picture old people talking like teenagers, and if it were up to me, I'd put a quick stop to it.

I mention this at dinner my first night at Marshall's house, and you know what? They all laugh, and it's so weird to hear people laughing at the dinner table that I feel really bad and stare into my plate, but Mrs. Hickler says, "No, Milo—that's really funny. My mother does act a little like she's still in high school. You should see her yoga clothes." And it's so shocking that laughing even coexists with eating, and it's while I'm having broiled chicken (which I love) and green beans (which I hate but eat anyway) that I want to go home and pack up all my stuff and move right into Marshall's house forever.

If I squint, I can pretend that I'm in a different kitchen with a different family—my family—and there's always laughing and sometimes yelling going on, but it's the kind of yells that end usually with hugs and sometimes pudding. Pudding with Reddi-wip, which I can spray straight into my mouth until the one time I nearly choke and then it's not allowed anymore and my mom never buys it again.

It's cool that my dad's agreed to let me sleep over at Marshall's house for two nights, which is something I normally would hate to do because I'm a one-night-only kind of sleepover guy, but three things make this a great decision:

1) It's the week between Christmas and New Year's.

2) My sister is gone at my house.

3) Marshall's house feels normal.

Normal houses are the houses you see on TV where people talk more than they don't talk and they eat together and play games like Uno or Crazy Eights even when they don't want to. These houses smell like brownies or chocolate chip cookies, and if you find a moldy half-eaten tuna sandwich in the cushion of the couch, it's an exception and not a rule.

Marshall's house is all that and more, and his mom is supernice to me, and his dad might be strange but he likes when I'm around and, after the first incident with the exploding pen, only asks if I want to try something he's working on if it doesn't involve electricity.

Last week when the phone rang and it was Marshall and he said, "Hi" and I said, "Hi" and then he said, "Can my mom talk to your dad?" I thought I was in trouble or something. But after my dad hung up and he looked at me not like I just broke his car window with a hammer (which was a total accident) but like he was glad about something, I thought that maybe I was being adopted.

"The Hicklers have invited you to stay at their house this week." And because he knows how I feel about sleepovers, he quickly added, "For *two* nights. What do you say?"

Inside I was saying, *Yes, get me out of here because it's just you and me and a lot of silence and frozen food.* But I looked in his face, and even though he was smiling, I thought his eyes were saying that he wanted me to stay behind and be with him. As much as I wanted to escape the house, I felt bad about leaving him behind.

But then I figured it's like in a movie when one prisoner gets a chance to escape and the other prisoner guy is wounded and insists that he won't make it and it's all up to you and you have to do it. You just have to!

And so I did. I escaped!

After dinner it's like the greatest night ever. First Marshall and I don't have to help clear the table and can go straight to his room and play video games. He has two controllers, so it works out great.

After that his mom and dad light a real fire in the fireplace (not one of those fake wrapped-in-paper logs) and then we get to roast marshmallows and make s'mores, which are these things I never heard of but most kids know about. Here's how they work:

The last thing that makes the night superspecial is that it starts to snow—and not just a little bit. You can tell just by looking out at the streetlights where the snowflakes are thick and falling hard and fast that this is going to be a snowstorm!

The only bummer part is that this is the exact kind of snow where you can start getting excited that they're canceling school tomorrow and you stay up listening to the little radio by your bed waiting for the announcement and you keep listening for the sound of the heavy plows on your street and you doze off a little at the end and when you wake up . . . it's your dad and there *is* school and you get really mad.

But it's vacation, so there won't be school tomorrow no matter what. And I'm at Marshall's and not at my house, where the snow will pile up higher than here and the rooms will feel colder even with the thermostat turned way up.

"Hey," Marshall says across the darkness of his room.

"Hey," I say back from the air mattress on the floor, which is actually way more comfortable than it looks and blows up by plugging it into the wall.

"This is great. You sleeping over."

"Yup. Way great." And I mean it. It's just the best.

"Milo," Marshall says, and I can tell he's getting

sleepy because the *o* in my name kind of falls off the edge of his bed and rolls around on the floor. "You think maybe Summer Goodman is . . ."

And I wait because I know how Marshall will finish that sentence, and in my mind I write the words for him in HUGE BOLD letters like this:

". . . IS TOTALLY GORGEOUS!"

But he doesn't speak, and then finally I have to clear my throat in that obvious throat-clearing-snot way, and Marshall starts again. But his words aren't what I'd pictured at all. He says, "Don't you think she's kind of . . . you know, a stuck-up snob?" And for a second his sentence gets all lit up in my head and it kicks and stomps on my sentence and his words make me mad.

How could he say something so bad about the girl I am in love with, who still doesn't know the real me . . . or the fake me . . . or any me at all?

We don't talk, and just the heavy metal sound of a snowplow outside pushing away the storm fills the space, and then it's like the plow pushes the words and feelings away too because suddenly I don't care what he just asked me.

And I close my eyes and picture Summer Goodman making snow angels with me, and even though I know she'd be the one to stomp through them with her boots, I still think she's the best thing ever.

snowed in

THE FIRST THING IS, I AM ASLEEP AND I am dreaming of being in the ocean and my dad is throwing me up in the air and then I splash down below the surface of the cold water, except it doesn't feel cold—it's real cozy. Underneath, the colors are different and with my eyes open, I see his legs standing solid against the waves and the light swirls the sand like small tornados.

Seaweed, coral, even the hairs on my dad's legs seem to individually wave at me, and it feels like I'm underwater forever, but then I pop above the surface and Mom's there too and together they grab my arms and twirl me around in circles and I don't get dizzy. I just look up past their smiles and the blue sky stares down at me, and suddenly I know it's a dream because someone else's voice is there too:

"Milo. Get up. You gotta see this."

And I have no choice because the ocean is gone and I know I'm in a bed, and then I remember I'm not in my own house and I let my eyes open and I'm looking up at Marshall's face.

His grin says it all, but his words confirm it: "It's a blizzard!"

I'm dressed in, like, two seconds, and we both tear down the stairs to the living room so we can look outside at the street. "Oh, man," I say.

And Marshall bounces up and down on the couch saying, "Double that!"

Outside the snow is piled up three and a half feet and it's still coming down.

We think up different things to do in snow like this:

- We want to build a fort—and not just an igloo kind of barrier to hide behind, but one with a real roof that we can stand inside and maybe sleep in if we wear enough layers.
- We plan to spend one full hour assembling a stockpile of snowballs for a snowball fight that will take forever to be finished. (We agree on no slush balls or iron rockets, which is when you put a rock in the middle of the snowball and it can take your eye out.)

• Sledding down Chamberlain Street is on the list because it's really steep and even the salt trucks have a hard time getting to it.

Dressed in layers that make moving nearly impossible, we wave good-bye and enter the snow, which reaches all the way up to my waist.

Our first paying job is Marshall's house, and it

takes half an hour to clear the walkway from the street to the front door. We each get five bucks, which may not sound like a lot but when your Freezie fund is down to two dollars and fifty cents and your Summer Goodman secret ring fund is wavering around one seventy-five, five bucks *each* feels pretty sweet.

"Okay," I announce. "My house next!"

We march off with shovels on our shoulders and end up on my street, and the biggest surprise of all is that my house is already done. My dad has paid someone with a plow and a snowblower, and there's nothing we can do but sit on my front steps and wish we'd skipped thinking anything at my house would work out okay.

My dad asks if we want to come in, but I know there'll be no hot chocolate or good snacks and I don't want to let go of the feeling I am on a vacation at Marshall's house, so I say no.

"Hey," Marshall says, pointing at something across the street. "That house isn't shoveled."

I look up and see that Marshall is talking about my weird old lady neighbor, who buys pumpkins too early and stands by her window waiting to wave at me all day.

I say, "Forget it. She's nuts." But Marshall won't forget it, so I have to follow him as he rushes across the street really fast because he's afraid some guy in a plow truck will swoop in and get the job first.

Once we finally climb the impossible snow-covered stairs, I kind of on purpose stand a bit back from Marshall as he rings the bell. I'm half hoping no one is home or that if she is home, she's too busy to come to the door, but those two half hopes disappear as soon as the door opens and there she is smiling and holding a cup of something steamy, which she tells us is mint tea.

Two things I notice right away: The weird old lady isn't old. Well, not in the "old lady" way I thought she was. Up close she's "teacher old," not "grandma old."

And the second thing is: She sees me right away, and even though we've never met, she says, "Hello,

Milo." And then, "So, what can I do for you boys?"

Marshall does the negotiating, and by the time he's done laying out our expertise and skill level, we've got the go-ahead. "However, I think ten dollars isn't a fair price for so much work," the old lady who isn't so old says. "Let's make it fifteen, and I'll throw in some snacks."

The door closes, and Marshall kicks snow at me. "You said she was crazy."

We work double hard mainly because it's later in the day and the snow, which started off light and powdery, is now heavy and wet and takes way more effort to actually lift. "If she tries to feed us, just say no. I don't trust her ingredients," I yell to Marshall, who answers back with a snowball that smacks my parka with a dull thud. Wearing so many layers, I don't even feel it. But I like the sound it makes.

The very last thing to do is the steps to her door, and I say that I'll do them even though I know once I finish, we'll have to go inside her house, which is starting to make me feel like I want to just go home.

"Almost finished," I shout down to Marshall, who is putting the finishing touches on the driveway.

"We are awesome!" he yells back. "And rich!"

And I agree with him because together we made twenty-five dollars, which isn't as much as our original hopes but still is enough money to do some serious Pit Stop damage.

I'm pushing the snow off the top step when I feel the metal shovel edge hit something solid. In my brain I wonder if I'm about to uncover a treasure or a body part—or more likely a package left in the snow that is now frozen solid. It takes me a second to realize (duh) that this is the welcome mat.

I chop at the caked-on snow with the steel tip of my shovel until I free the mat from the cement. But the mat is still trapped in a layer of frozen snow, so I decide the best thing to do is to lift the whole thing up and then drop it so that the rest of the snow will crack off. It's a lot heavier than I thought, but I get it up over my head and then let the mat fall hard against the top step. And as soon as it hits, I freeze because the thing doesn't say WELCOME on it. It says HOME, and there's something about seeing that word staring back at me that makes me feel warm and cold at the same time.

And that's when the door opens—and the weird lady is standing there smiling out from the inside saying, "Great job!" And then she says, "Come on in."

She's holding two steaming mugs of something,

which of course has to be hot chocolate even though she calls it "cocoa," and then Marshall is right next to me and he's smiling so I smile too, even though for some reason I don't want to.

I find it a little strange to actually be on the *inside* of the weird lady's house, especially because I have spent all year looking the other way every time I see her and ignoring her waves at me.

Boots off. Snow pants, too. We are finally free of the winter armor, and that alone is cause for celebration. The lady hands us the cups of "cocoa" and she's put marshmallows on top and they are already turned gooey.

"You two sure work hard," she says, showing us to the kitchen, where I smell the cookies before I even know they exist. And I see she's used a store-bought kind where you just slice the dough from a log, but I smile anyway because I can tell they taste good just by looking at the plate of chocolate chip cookies on the table.

"I hope you boys are hungry," she says, and even though I really am, I try to pretend I'm not. Marshall doesn't pretend anything, and two cookies are already in his mouth. It's a small kitchen painted yellow, which is one of those colors that I hate. The fridge is covered in lists and funny magnets and a few drawings obviously done by a kid of some kind.

"My grandkids love to send me pictures," she says, almost like she's reading my mind, which creeps me out.

I look away, hoping to break off her mind-vibe powers, and I stare at the wall next to where we sit instead. I'm amazed the whole wall is covered with framed pictures, and they are mostly photographs of the lady and a man, who are standing in different places all around the world.

"That's me and my husband," she says. She points to the picture closest to my face. "That's Paul and me in Paris. And that one," she says, pointing to the picture next to it, "that one is in Cairo."

"Cairo. Cool," Marshall says, filling his mouth with another cookie, and only I know he has no clue where Cairo is, which is Egypt.

I just nod and keep scanning the wall of pictures, and I can't believe she would waste so much time putting so many pictures in one place. The thing that really gets me is that every picture is the same: Just the two of them standing in one place or another. Sure, they're different ages in some of them; but otherwise, the whole wall could be one picture of two people just with different backgrounds.

There's lots of pictures, and as I try to guess where on a map each photo was taken, I feel the lady isn't looking at the picture wall anymore but at me, and turning around, I see that I am right. She's watching me, so I quickly say, "Where is the bathroom?" And then off I go.

Sometimes I say I have to "go" because I really need to; and sometimes I say it when I just want to get away for a minute, and that is this kind of time.

Inside the bathroom the wallpaper is shiny like tin foil and it has a flowery smell that is definitely old-lady smell, but that's no surprise. The toilet seat is covered in a flowered cushiony thing that I don't want to touch, which makes me thankful I don't really have to use it.

I know I can't stay in here too long, so I flush the toilet and then go to wash my hands so the lady won't think I'm one of those gross germy kids you see on TV commercials. I see that the soap dish is full of those tiny seashell soaps that smell weird and are impossible to actually use, so I just wet my hands in the sink, and because the hand towel looks brand new, I wipe my wet hands on my pants and then I go back to the kitchen.

"I dunno. I think pretty good," I hear Marshall saying to the lady who has taken my chair, and as soon as they see me, they both stop talking, which I think means I am either in trouble or they were talking about me.

"Well, Milo," she says, getting out of my chair. "I guess the time has come."

And I have no idea what she means, but I am hoping it means it's time to get out of there. But all that happens is she holds out her hand, and I see it's just a little bit wrinkly and I guess I stare at the veins just a little too long because the next thing is, I hear her voice. "I'm Sylvia. Sylvia Poole."

And she waits until I figure out she's waiting for

my hand, so I quickly wipe it again on my pants just in case it's still a little wet, and then I put my hand in hers and say, "I'm Milo." Which is way dumb because she obviously knows that.

She smiles. "There. We did it. Now maybe when I say hello, you can say hi back." She winks, which seems kind of creepy, but I still hold her hand and it's warm and not in a way that makes me want to let go. "But if you don't say hi . . . that's okay too."

"Oh, man!" Marshall sees the wall clock and freaks out. It's after four, so we quickly put our snow clothes back on, and if you ever had to wear snow pants and big boots, you know that it takes a ton of time to get those things back on, especially after you have just had cookies and cocoa.

Sylvia gives us the extra cookies all wrapped up in foil, and then she dials Marshall's mom on the phone and says we are on our way and that it was her fault we are late, which actually was a cool thing for her to do. "Don't be strangers!" she calls to us before closing the door.

And the last thing I see before we grab our shovels and run all the way back to Marshall's house—where we have just heard it is meat loaf and applesauce night—is the word on the welcome mat, the word that welcomes me back anytime I want:

new year's baby

THE TWO-NIGHT VACATION AT MARSHALL'S goes by way too fast, and it's strange to be back in my own house again, which is the reverse of how it's supposed to be.

I try talking to my dad. Sort of, anyway. "How's it going?" I ask him while he sits at the kitchen table doing a crossword puzzle in the newspaper.

"Fantastic," he says back without looking. "I hope you had a great time."

"It was pretty okay." I don't go into any details because I don't want to tell him how good it felt being someplace that wasn't here. All I add is, "We had waffles."

Silence.

"Four-letter word for Norse god. Any guesses?" I watch him chew the pencil tip while he scans the kitchen as if the answer is written in special ink and hidden next to the cupboards or by the sink. "Four letters. 'O,' blank, 'I,' blank."

But I'm blank too and just shrug, feeling like I've let him down somehow.

"Your sister called," he says, already filling in some other empty boxes with letters that will eventually make sense. "She said she misses you."

And I laugh inside because I know two things: (1) My dad is the one who did the calling, and (2) my sister is in Florida with a friend from school and the last thing she is missing is me.

But I don't say anything except, "Cool."

The doorbell rings. My dad and I look at each other with the same puzzled stare, and I swear we both want to hide under the kitchen table—but maybe that's just me.

The bell rings again. Twice. *Ding. Diiiing.*

My dad turns to me:

So I shuffle off to see who it is.

It's cold in the small entrance hall and I want to get this over with fast, so I swing the door open and it's Hillary Alpert standing outside my door and she holds a small package and it's wrapped in green tissue paper, so instantly I know I am in trouble because I am sure it is for me.

"Hey, Milo," she says, smiling. "We just got back."

And I have to search the part of my brain that holds on to useless information, but no lightbulbs go off. I really have no idea what she is talking about, so I just stare at her and watch her breath make small cotton-ball clouds in the freezing night air.

She tries to give me clues just like my dad and his crossword. "From vacation. Remember? My cousins in Texas?"

And then I remember the last note she gave me right before school ended, and I can say a normal thing like, "Terrific."

She steps inside all on her own, and secretly I'm glad because my toes have gone numb and I'm sure I have frostbite, which means they will have to be cut off before morning.

"I got you something. Hope it's okay."

And now she hands me the green tissue paper thing, and I quickly look around the entrance hallway where we stand to try to find something I can give her back, but all I see are two mismatched gloves, yesterday's newspaper, and a tennis ball that Patches has chewed so much that it looks like it has a pink bald spot where the yellow fuzzy stuff used to be.

Reluctantly, I take her gift and can feel that whatever is inside is small and light, but there's no way I can open it. "I don't have anything for you." I feel about an inch tall and wish she would disappear and take her present away with her unless it's something I might actually want—in which case I'd be happy to hold on to it for safekeeping.

"No biggie. It's just something stupid." She smiles, and I see that the tip of her nose is all red from the cold. "I saw it and thought of you. That's all."

My first thought is that she said it was something *stupid* . . . and it reminded her of *me*. Great. But then I open it and see it's one of those plastic snow-globe things that you shake and then watch the snow swirl inside. What makes this one funny is that inside the plastic globe it's not a ski slope or the Empire State Building. It says TEXAS SNOWMAN, and all that's inside is water and a small plastic carrot and a top hat.

It takes me a second to get it, because my first thought is you can't make a snowman in Texas.

"Wow, Hillary. It's really funny." And I mean it too. "Next time I go anywhere, I'm definitely getting you something stupid."

"Okay," she says. And then, "I have to get home. I just wanted to give you the present."

I look down at the snow globe and shake it up. The carrot and hat swirl around inside kind of like they are chasing each other. Then I look back at Hillary. "Thanks again. It's awesome."

She nods and pulls her down coat tighter as she gets ready to face the cold. She opens my front door and then pushes herself into the winter air. "Oh yeah," she calls back right before I close my door. "Happy New Year."

And it hits me that it's New Year's Eve, and suddenly I feel like the snowman inside the globe as I melt into myself because I hate New Year's Eve and had somehow managed to escape remembering what day it was.

"Uh, yeah," I shout back. "Happy New Year to you, too."

And then I close the door and let the quiet of my house swallow me up—because I know that everywhere else in the world people are making noise and dancing and going crazy with the excitement of welcoming a whole new year instead of filling in the blanks with a chewed-over pencil.

I go up to my room and look at the clock by my bed. 10:45 it blinks at me. I put the Texas snowman on my dresser and wish it were tomorrow already. I think about how if I could fly my own jet, I could totally avoid New Year's Eve by crossing different time zones just to skip the actual second the old year ends and the new one begins.

10:46.

But I can't really avoid the countdown, which by my calculations is still one hour and fourteen minutes away.

As years go, the old one has been not too awful. I've got a cool best friend who likes the same weird stuff as me, and I still have all my hair, unlike Mr. Shivnesky's head. The way I see things, the new year is full of possibilities, like it's *possible* I will make honor roll. It's *possible* Marshall and I will finally beat Warfighter 4 on his Xbox, and it's *possible* that Summer Goodman and I will have a moment where she sees how perfect we'd be together.

These things all could happen. And knowing this tips the scales in favor of the new year.

Bring it on, I tell myself, knowing that anything is possible now!

Lying on my bed, a memory of New Year's Eve comes to me, and I see my family, the four of us sitting by the TV wearing those silly hats and holding party noisemakers in our hands. There are special snacks like tiny hotdogs soaked in a grape jelly sauce that you have to eat with toothpicks, and bowls of potato chips and an onion dip my mom and sister made from a mix. We watched the Times Square party on TV and I felt like I was the oldest kid in the world staying up until midnight and doing this together—all of us.

10 . . . 9 . . . 8 . . . 7 . . . 6 . . . 5 . . . 4 . . . 3 . . . 2 . . .

And we all shouted "Happy New Year!" and threw confetti and blew the noisemakers and it was just like being with all those party people on TV, only way better because it was our family that was hugging and laughing as the old year gave way to a new one that instantly felt shiny and perfect.

And then I remember that was the new year that became the worst year—the year she got sick and the year the fog came.

10:47.

I lean over to my clock and use the up and down buttons to make the digital numbers race ahead until it tells me the time is 12:01.

"Happy New Year," I say to the melted snowman, whose missing smile agrees with my choice to zoom around the globe and beat the New Year's Baby at his own game.

silent treatment

SOMETIMES A WHOLE SUPPER CAN GO by and the only words that get said are "May I please be excused?"

Okay. Maybe *some* words get said. Like, my dad might say, "More peas?" or "Wow, this is one juicy piece of steak."

I don't blame my dad for all the quiet. My sister doesn't exactly say stuff either. I kind of keep my words stuffed inside the food that's being chewed around in my mouth. I just can't think of what to say that doesn't sound wrong, which is why it's just way easier to settle into the silence of one of the three suppers my dad knows how to make:

- meat loaf
- spaghetti and meatballs
- steaks

Dinner used to be a circus. My mom loved to cook with the radio playing, and it always had to be music, which meant oldies or classical or even country-western songs. She didn't care as long as it was loud and something you could make a chicken leg dance to.

Everything was stirred together: mixing bowls, pans hitting the counter, her singing along with the radio even without knowing the words while the Beatles wanted to hold her hand or some other guy wanted to do the twist. And if she couldn't find a certain knife or the measuring cup wasn't in the right spot, she'd tear the place apart searching for the missing thing, which usually was being played with by me on the floor.

My mom had a dozen different aprons, and each one was sillier than the next: Hawaii Apron. Daisies Apron. Dogs Chase Cats Apron. Kiss the Cook Apron. Sitting in the kitchen while she got supper ready, I'd close my eyes and try to guess which apron she was wearing, and even though I always guessed wrong, it was the game that was the fun part.

"Milo, help me measure," she'd always ask, and I felt bigger than the refrigerator every time using the tablespoon that jingled next to the other measuring spoons all held together by the silver key ring.

"Not too much oil, honey," she'd say, holding my hand to make sure nothing spilled, and it was never like we did any of this because we wanted to eat—it was more like we just liked being together.

"Now mix the eggs with the sugar," and I would do it with the flat wooden spoon my dad would later just throw away.

It was her idea to have "upside-down suppers," where you start with dessert and then eat backward to the appetizer course. And she was the one who gave both my sister and me one night a month where we could plan the dinner menu—and she'd make it no matter if we chose cookie dough casserole or chicken à la chocolate.

Back then the kitchen was never dull and boring and was always in between one meal and the next, and I'd give anything to bring that noise back into our lives.

2 good 2 b 4-gotten

"I'M TELLING YOU, MILO. DON'T DO IT," MARSHALL says, but I think I know better mainly because I have already stayed up way past midnight putting my carefully laid-out plan in motion.

It's Valentine's Day, and I am ready to let my heart speak for me instead of keeping a huge piece of tape over its mouth.

This is why I am standing in the cafeteria holding the following items:

1) An oversized homemade card

2) A plastic rose that cost a buck at the Pit Stop

3) A piece of stationery (fancy) with my own poem on it

4) A heart-shaped box of chocolates with only one piece missing because Marshall didn't know it was for Summer, and it was caramel

I don't care that it's Tuna-Noodle Casserole Day. My stomach is all nervous, which is because of all the excitement about finally telling Summer Goodman how I feel. I wait until she is at her favorite table by the window, and then I walk over and say the thing I have practiced in the mirror.

"Happy Valentine's Day, Summer." I'm impressed that the words come out exactly as rehearsed, which is the last thing that goes as planned.

All of a sudden, instead of hearing her say *Oh, Milo* my ears are ringing with Summer laughing really hard. And loud.

"You're kidding me, right?" is what she is saying to me, and I don't know where I can go to hide or disappear from sight forever.

Dabney St. Claire says love is blind, so I guess I have some excuse because I probably need a new prescription for my glasses, but I really should start listening to Marshall because he never has moments like these in front of the whole cafeteria where a girl or *anyone* laughs so loud that even the teacher on duty, who usually doesn't notice anything, stops picking the meat loaf stain off his jacket and stares at the reason for the ruckus—which is YOU.

I just wish I could rewind the tape and do it all over, but not with Summer—with a girl who would react right, and that could mean lots of different ways, not just the most obvious.

And right now—after the laughter finally is down to a giggle and kids have stopped staring at me and I can sort of feel my face not being bright red anymore—you know what I miss the most? It isn't my mom, though of course she's in the top two. What I miss the most is it being Valentine's Day and opening my lunch box and finding a pink frosted cupcake with cinnamon hearts that spell out the words I LUV YOU.

That's what she did. Every year. Just for me. And right now I'd give anything to find that cupcake—or *any* cupcake—in my lunch, but since I buy lunch every day, the closest thing to a pink frosted cupcake is a square of stale cake with cracked yellow frosting and an ancient candy heart on top that looks like it would break your tooth if you dared bite into it.

There's only one logical choice: I have to escape! So I go to the office, grab my stomach, and say, "Uooogh. I think I feel sick."

"That's too bad," Mrs. Cranston, who is the lady who answers the phones and hands out late slips, says. "Too many Valentine's Day sweets, huh, buddy?"

I answer her question with a nod, even though it's a lie. My stomach is burning from not enough sweets.

A phone call to my dad later, I am riding the bus home, staring out the window and wishing I had two parents so one of them could pick me up when I need a ride home in the middle of the day. Of course, I wish that the other parent would be my mom, but at times like this I almost think it could be anyone with a valid driver's license and access to a car.

Settling in for the ride home, I look around and make a list of some of the people who ride the 138 bus in the middle of a Tuesday afternoon:

- Two old ladies wearing bulky coats that make me think they are hiding whole chickens or babies
- A businessman listening to an iPod (which just seems weird), and it has to be *classical* music even though he is tapping his foot fast

- The mom with her baby, who has decided to start crying—maybe because he knows about the smuggled babies hidden in the old ladies' coats

● Weird guy, who carries a huge garbage bag of something that smells as bad as he does, and he is talking to the invisible friend next to him

The cool thing that hits me is this: Not counting the screaming baby, whose face looks like it wants to explode, *I am the only kid on the bus!*

Three stops later I have a choice to make because we are about to be at the Pit Stop and I could get off here and buy something junk-foody for the ten-minute walk back home, or I could stay on the bus and then only have to walk from the top of my street to my house. It's a no-brainer and I pull the cord above me.

As soon as the bus pulls away, I realize it's wicked

cold outside and maybe stopping for the candy was a bad idea, which doesn't matter now that I'm standing here shivering in the parking lot, so I push against the wind and make my way to the oasis of the Pit Stop.

Inside I notice two things right away:

1) Awful, loud music isn't playing on the radio behind the counter.

2) Pete is also not behind the counter.

"Where's Pete?" I ask the lady smoking a cigarette, even though there are signs everywhere that say NO SMOKING.

"Who's Pete?" she says, blowing smoke right at me, which I avoid by holding my breath until all the smoke clears because secondhand smoke kills.

"Pete runs the Pit Stop. Do you work for him?"

This must be a funny thing because the lady laughs so hard, she ends up coughing, and it's that juicy, hacking smoker's cough that sounds like maybe a piece of her is about to come flying out if she can't stop. So I take two steps back just in case. Luckily, she stops one hack short of her lungs popping out.

"Kid," she says, "you're in Pit Stop number 342. I think you want Pit Stop number 281 down on Chandler Street. I'm pretty sure some guy named Pete works there."

Of course! I'm such a knucklehead! There are two Pit Stops on my bus ride home, and I am so used to riding the bus sitting with Marshall and not old ladies and screaming babies and businessmen with iPods that I got off at the first one instead of the second one, and now I'm really far from my house.

"Milo?" I turn and see it's Sylvia Poole, my crazy old lady neighbor who isn't crazy or old. "Aren't you supposed to be in school?" She asks this maybe a little too much like she thinks I'm skipping school or something bad.

"Got sick," I say. "Stomachache." Then I watch her eyes and they look down at my hand, which is clutching a Cruncho caramel candy bar I picked up when I walked into the store. "Um, I'm better now."

Sylvia nods and now the smile is there. "Well, I'm just getting a few ingredients and then heading back home. Want a lift?"

And I do want a lift—but I wish it were with the invisible person who won't ask me a ton of questions and not with her because she smiles a lot and seems nice but will probably yak nonstop. Of course, weighing out the weight of my backpack and the long freezing walk home versus sitting in her warm car and answering a few dumb questions, I have to make the smart choice and say, "Why not?"

Driving home isn't that bad because instead of asking me anything, she tells me things: "I just got back from a trip to China," she says.

I nod my head.

"It was amazing. All the pictures you see—they just don't even come close to what's really there."

"I bet." This is as easy as riding with my dad.

She starts talking about the Great Wall and how Chinese food in China isn't at all like going to the Beijing Palace All-You-Can-Eat Buffet down by the bus station, and I listen politely, which means smiling but not really hearing.

And then I sneak a look in her plastic Pit Stop bag that sits between us and see a small bag of cinnamon hearts and a can of pink frosting, and suddenly all I want to do is talk.

disappearing act

IT MUST BE A WEEK THAT GOES BY BEFORE I'm unpacking my school bag and find a small envelope stuck inside my Spanish book with my name on it. *Milo.*

Of course, my first thought is that Summer Goodman has written a Valentine apology, and after

I cross my arms and think *Nothing you can say will undo my pain,* I get so excited, I am almost shaking inside.

But even Dabney St. Claire tells me to hold my horses. And so I take a closer look at the small envelope and see that the handwriting doesn't match how Summer always writes, with bright colored pens she carries in a tiny green case with her name written in gold marker on the side.

The envelope just says *Milo* and the pen is nothing special and I'm kind of scared to solve the mystery because what if it's a note telling me I have a disease?

I slide my finger under the part of the envelope that isn't sticky and tear the top enough so I can get inside. Pulling the card out, I see it's a note card. With a flower on it. I hold my breath because I know in a second the mystery of who sent it will be solved, and then I count to three . . . and open the card.

It's from my across-the-street neighbor, who must've slipped it inside my bag the other day—Valentine's Day, when I was in her house.

Eating a warm cupcake decorated with pink frosting and cinnamon hearts, Sylvia Poole tells me about her husband, Paul.

"Paul loved the beach." . . . "Paul had a thing for pomegranates." . . . "If anyone could ruin a song by singing it out loud, it was Paul."

She just can't stop telling me about the man who is in all those pictures on her kitchen wall, and to be honest, I don't mind listening. It's Valentine's Day and the cupcakes are still gooey, and besides, I don't have a house key so it's a lucky thing to be stuck in her warm old-lady house instead of freezing my butt off waiting for my sister to get out of school.

I'm in the middle of my second cupcake when I hear, "Do you miss your mom, Milo?" And I stop mid-chew because her question comes at me from left field, and as good as everything tastes, I suddenly want to be anywhere else in the whole world but in this moment.

I can't look at her, so instead I look down at the table and stare at the plate and focus really hard to make sure that's all that I see. Luckily, I don't have to answer her because she's the next one to talk.

"I miss Paul," she says. "He sure loved Valentine's Day. What a sweetie."

My eyes work overtime to keep staring at my plate, which is white but has a blue stripe around the edge and the cupcake crumbs are all scattered within the circle.

I sense that Sylvia is now sitting down at the table with me, and I feel trapped and there's no way I can leave without talking, and talking is something that right now feels impossible. And even though

I promised myself I wouldn't, I look up from the plate and see this lady I hardly know is crying.

Soft. Slow. But definitely crying.

"Oh, did we have some fun times," she is saying, maybe to me or maybe to the photographs. I can't tell. She lifts the corner of the apron she wears and dabs her wet eyes twice.

Her eyes catch mine, which was a mistake on my part—but once the deed is done, I look back and see that she is actually smiling. And it's weird that she looks so happy even with eyes that have just cried.

"He was a good man, Milo," she sighs. "And I miss him every day."

In my brain I say something just to myself, but I make the mistake of also saying it out loud: "How could you not miss him every day. He's everywhere you look!"

For a second I worry this sounds a little snotty, so I gaze up at the Wall of Paul, and even I miss him a little bit even though I've never met him.

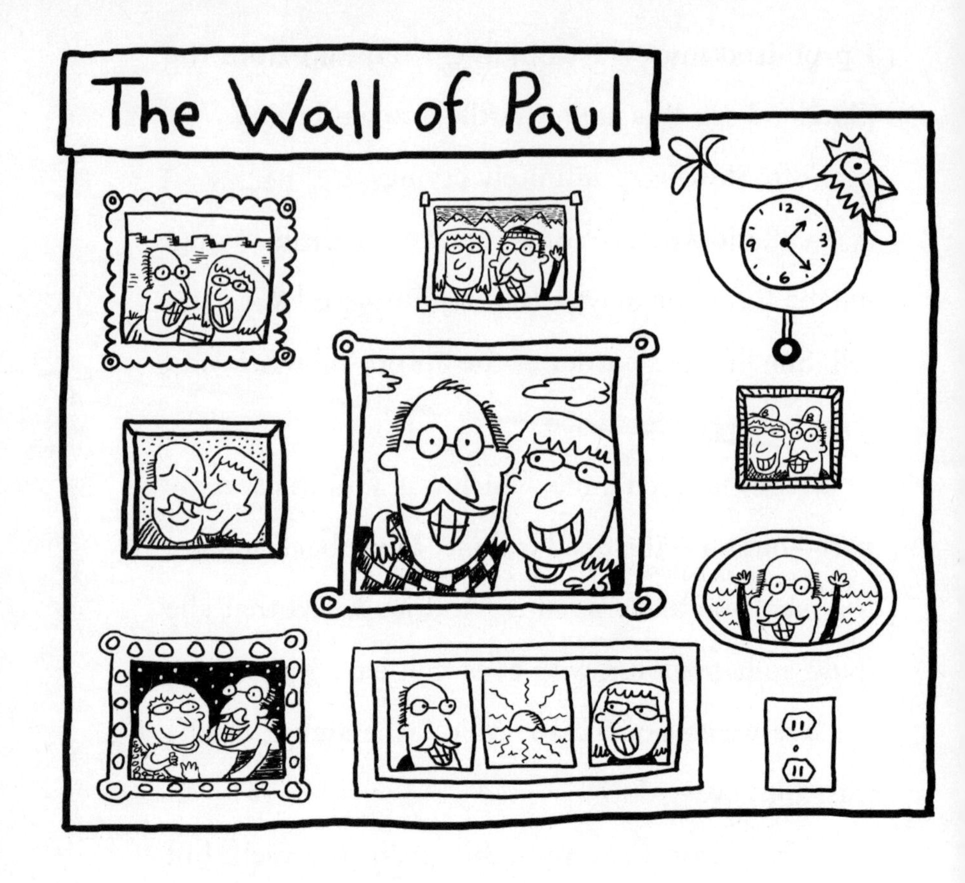

Sylvia smiles and I can tell she is done crying. "I want him to be everywhere I look. I want to remember him. All the time, Milo. All the time."

I nod.

"And you know what else, Milo?"

I don't. So I say nothing.

"That's how I keep him alive. By making sure I think about him every day."

I am on the edge of my chair partly because I want to say something and partly because I want to escape. Dabney St. Claire nudges me. *Say it*, he tells me, and so I ease back fully onto the red vinyl cushion and follow his advice.

"Truth is," I say in a small voice, "I don't really remember a ton about her. Just that she's gone."

"Oh, Milo," Sylvia says to me as she looks at my face from across the table with such kindness that I quickly inspect the floor for anything but words. "That must feel like being lost somewhere between one place and another."

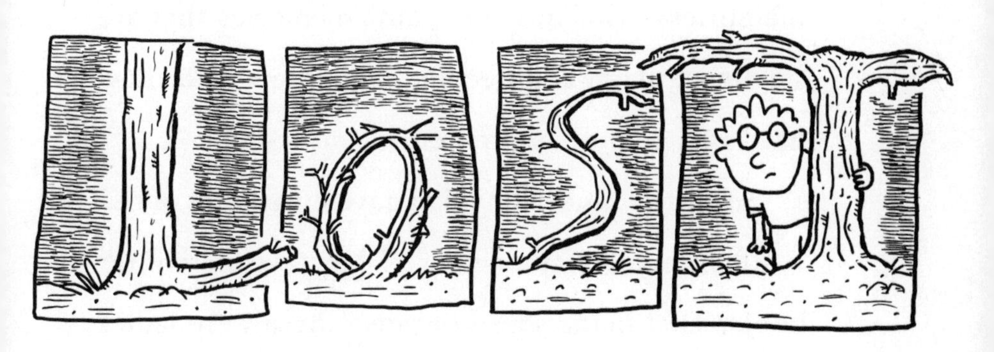

• • •

I'm now sitting on my bed holding the card from Sylvia Poole, reading the words again that she obviously wants me to have: *Don't forget her.*

At first it makes me mad that Sylvia slipped this message to me, but then I picture all of the photographs inside her kitchen and all of the stories she told me and I can feel how alive her dead husband is while my dead mother is just dead.

And I'm flooded with wanting to look at pictures of us as a family or to hold some of her broken jewelry or to wrap myself in her smell—but I know that there's nothing left. It's all been given away or sold or thrown in the garbage, leaving only memories—real "in your brain" memories that are starting to fade and become fuzzy no matter how hard I try to hold on to them.

After the funeral my dad gave away a lot of her stuff. Dresses, hats, a pair of her favorite winter boots. That made sense because there were ladies who were poor and didn't have things. And that's why he called one of those places that come to your house to take away the garbage bags full of clothes and then give them to people who need what you no longer do.

Soon after that I'd see ladies walking around in the supermarket or in the mall and I'd look real hard to see if any of them were wearing her stuff, and I guess I was secretly hoping I'd get to see a piece of my mom roaming around like she was still around, only in someone else's body. But I never saw anyone wearing my mom's ghost clothes, and pretty soon I stopped thinking about it.

The clothes giveaway seemed like a good idea, and even though I missed seeing her fuzzy bathrobe and long winter coat and other Mom-clothes around the house, I didn't really care. But my dad started getting rid of other stuff, too. A whole set of dishes disappeared—and it was the set with the flower pattern around the edges that looked like spaceships if you mashed your creamed corn on top . . . and then some of the paintings in frames we used to have weren't there . . . and even a shaggy rug that used to be in front of the TV went away one day while I was at school.

"What's up?" I asked my sister, who knew everything back then.

"Dad's cleaning the house of Mom," she told me. "He's making her disappear."

By the time we'd moved from the Fog House into House #5, every one of our family portraits—even the cheesy one we did at Sears, where the backdrop was blue clouds and we all wore fake smiles—all of them were gone too. Then he bought new pots and pans without even thinking about all the meals we ate together that got cooked in the old ones, and then the silverware went missing too. *The silverware!*

Don't forget her, Sylvia tells me.

And I wonder how I can keep my mom from fading away when everything that reminds me of her is already gone.

Don't forget her.

But I feel like I already am, and I search my mind for all the things we no longer have that connect her to me.

burned popcorn

IT'S FRIDAY NIGHT, AND MARSHALL, HILLARY, and I decide to rent a DVD, which means Hillary's dad drives us to the Movie Scene. That's the video store that's located next to Los Tacos, a Mexican restaurant that makes all the movies smell like *arroz con pollo*, which is rice with chicken, which I know from learning *"Me llamo Milo. Yo gusto arroz con pollo. ¿Dónde está la biblioteca?"*

Hillary's dad doesn't come in with us. He just waits in the car listening to a book on tape, something I don't quite understand because I see he has the paperback version right there on the dashboard. Hillary says that's because after every book-on-tape chapter, he likes to stop and read those pages to make sure the guy reading the book out loud doesn't skip any of the good parts.

Even though it almost makes sense, I decide he is way weird.

We wander the aisles, and it takes us about forty-five minutes to come to some decision that doesn't include anything with too much blood or the undead (which Hillary says is a deal breaker).

"I want a comedy," she says.

"Things that go BOOM!" Marshall is excited.

"No subtitles." This is my demand.

We go for a classic—*Galaxy Quest*, which is a really funny outer-space movie in a dumb kind of way.

"This one's on me," Marshall says, strutting all the way up to the bored-looking teenager at the cash register. "Birthday cash stash!"

Back in the car we realize it's time to decide whose house has the best "Triple Threat." The Triple Threat is the system you use to decide where you are actually going to *watch* the DVD, and it boils down to three important things:

It's a no-brainer about the snacks issue because my house never has good stuff, mostly because my dad never buys any. Hillary reminds us she's allowed three nonhealthy snacks a week, so right away you know her house will have just apples and nuts, and that leaves Marshall, whose mom stocks the place to the roof with artificial colors and flavors.

As for butt comfort, it's Hillary's house hands down. TV size, too, because they have a whole room just for watching stuff, and it's got a wide-screen TV in it and a really great couch and a matching chair that swivels in circles.

"Snacks over TV," I say, already hungry for the sight of Marshall's cupboard, where the cupcakes and licorice twists are calling to me.

"Can't do it," Marshall says. "I just remembered my folks are having friends over to play cards or something dumb like that. Who plays cards, anyway?"

Hillary turns to her dad. "Can we watch it at our house?"

There's a second of hesitation on her father's part, which can only mean one thing: No way. And his excuse for it is totally lame: "Your mother and I have plans to watch a global warming documentary on the big TV. You kids can go in the basement, though."

We all shudder at the thought of Hillary's basement, where we have to sit on old beanbag chairs and watch a TV about the size of my math book. I suspect he knows this, and I am seething inside because by default we are stuck with my house.

"Well, look at this. A cinemania club," my dad says a little too loud as we settle into my den. He just stands there and I want him to go away, which I tell him with my eyes, but he either can't see or doesn't care because he starts doing weird stuff like offering to make popcorn and go get pizza. "Thanks but no thanks," I say, but Hillary's and Marshall's surprised faces make me revise my mind, and so I add, "I mean, it's okay if you *want* to."

Dabney St. Claire wants pepperoni, but Hillary is a vegetarian and Marshall says vegetables are against his religion so we have to settle on just cheese.

My dad writes it all down on a piece of paper and bows like he's a waiter, and I just want to be invisible. "Be back in twenty minutes," he says, which is a relief because now we can start the movie in peace.

While the previews play, Hillary taps my shoulder. "Your dad is nice."

And all I can do is shrug.

The movie starts, and we turn off all the lights and sink into the quicksand of my couch. As promised, twenty minutes into *Galaxy Quest*, my dad's back, and he bought bottles of grape and orange soda. I admit the movie gets better after the pizza arrives, and watching my friends thank my dad makes me think maybe what he did is a good thing and not the embarrassing thing I feel.

"Never give up! Never surrender!" That's the catchphrase in this movie, and every time the main character says it, Marshall stands up on my couch and says it too. The first time he does, grape soda comes out of Hillary's nose. The second time, we all laugh so hard that I have to pause the movie and then rewind it so all three of us can stand on the couch and yell it out too. "Never give up! Never surrender!"

Bowls of bad microwave popcorn appear from the man dressed up as my dad, and I apologize a bunch of times to my friends for having the cheap kind that never fully pops and is made with fake butter that smells a little like stale milk.

Hillary and Marshall just yell "Shut up!" enough times that I finally see their point that talking during the best scenes just ruins the movie, and I shut up and grab a handful of popcorn and slide into the feeling that I'm hanging out with friends on a Friday night, which instantly creates a check in one of my "Life Goals" boxes.

Truth is, I've hung out with Marshall tons on weekend nights, but that doesn't really count beyond the fact that Marshall is awesome and my best friend. With the addition of Hillary, the whole thing changes, and it's not because I like her, which I don't! It's because now it doesn't feel like two guys alone watching things explode on TV, it's three *friends*, which is a perfect number for meeting my goal and the reason the box gets checked now and not before.

MY LIFE GOALS

☑ #39: Weekends mean hanging out with friends

"Special features!" Marshall shouts when the movie is done. He loves all the goofy outtakes and documentary stuff that shows behind the scenes.

After we watch every special feature on the disc, we decide that life should have special features so you could learn about the behind-the-scenes stuff that goes on with all of us. We start a discussion that goes like this:

Marshall: "Okay, if you clicked on my special features button, you'd get to learn about how my mom once dressed me up as a dog for our Christmas card photo. The guy at the store even gave me a fake bone to hold. True story."

Hillary: "No way!"

Me: "It's true. I saw the picture. Funny."

Marshall: "Way funny."

Everyone: (laughs)

Hillary: "Well, if I had special features, I guess it'd be behind the scenes of when I used to name my fingernail clippings."

Marshall: "Whoa! That's pretty weird."

Hillary: "Really weird."

Me: "You think that's weird? What about this one: Hillary still has a whole shoe box of broken doll pieces that she hides under her bed!"

Marshall: "No way!"

Marshall finds this so strange that it's funny, and he starts rolling around on my floor like he's on fire. I laugh too because I want to be like Marshall—but then I see Hillary, who isn't even smiling, and my laughing voice evaporates.

"Oh, dude," Marshall says after his laughing dries up. "Now I gotta go to the bathroom." He gets up, leaving me alone with Hillary.

"I can't believe you, Milo." She is really mad. "That was a secret. I shared it with you. And you just made fun of it . . . of me."

I want to say I'm sorry, but that

part of me gets overtaken by the other part—the part that has just let all the air out of the fun and is trying to ruin everything. "What's the big deal?" that me says. "Those broken dolls were just stupid, anyway."

Hillary's eyes go from angry darts at me to sad mirrors, and there's nothing I can say or do to make that look go away. "Oh, really? Then why did you take one of them when you left?"

I forgot about that—and then I remember what I did and I blurt it out. "That stupid guy? I threw the pieces out my window. That's how dumb I thought he was." Wow, I can't believe I am being this mean.

Hillary stops looking at me and her eyes now watch my floor. Maybe she's hoping the conversation can be rewound like a DVD—that's what I'm hoping, anyway.

"I thought . . ." She can't even finish that sentence because she grabs her coat and walks out of my house.

Marshall comes back from the bathroom, and he's clueless that the Friday night we had a minute ago is now something totally else. He jumps onto my couch and strikes the catchphrase pose. "Let's watch it again!" He's pumped and up for anything.

But I can't do it. I am giving up and surrendering to the fact that I am a complete jerk.

salt and pepper

I LIKE MARCH BECAUSE IT'S JUST ONE CALENDAR page away from April, which is when the *real* spring weather hits. What I don't like is you just can't count on March: One day you get a warm breeze and the flowers start to wake up, and the next you get a snow day from school and your dad skids in a doughnut in the icy parking lot (which you actually think is fun, not dangerous, though it's both).

Totally unpredictable. That's March, which is why it makes me nervous.

Sylvia waves from her living room window, and as soon as I see her, I don't hesitate to wave back. I pretend I can't find my house key and turn to face her house, where she is already motioning me to come over.

Inside she asks how school was and what I'm up to and comments on my shirt, which has a big stain on it from art class where Barry Durwood decided I'd make a good canvas for his painting of a shark. And he got detention.

I saw Hillary just once today, and maybe that was because she was avoiding me and maybe it was because I did everything I could to walk the other way if I saw her. There were no purple notes in my locker today—or all last week for that matter—and I miss them. Even the stupid ones that just said hi.

"Gin!" Sylvia spreads all her cards out in that winning way that makes me admit I am not much of a cardplayer.

"I think I'm much more of a Crazy Eights kind of guy," I say to her as I push the cards back into a mishmash crash scene and then shuffle them as best I can.

"Don't underestimate your skills, Milo. You're already better than last time."

We play cards while the brownies finish baking and I wait for my sister or my dad to show up across the street, which will force me to admit I have to go back to my own house.

"Oh, I just remembered something," Sylvia says to me, and then leaves the kitchen. Quickly.

I kill the time she's gone by playing action

heroes with her salt and pepper shakers. The salt is a rooster and the pepper a hen, and I hold one in each hand while I make them fight each other in a monster movie called *Battle to the Death*. Salt-Rooster is the enemy who can turn anything it pours itself on into stone, and Pepper-Hen is the nemesis with the sprinkled power of extreme itchiness.

Right after they join forces to destroy the napkin holder, I finally notice that Sylvia is back, watching me. Smiling. "Paul used to love that silly rooster," she says. "For the life of me I don't know why."

And then easy as saying my name I add, "My mom had a set that was a cat and a dog. I think the dog was the salt."

Sylvia smiles again. "See that? Things attach to memories, Milo. It doesn't take much to remember, does it?"

And she's right, because thinking about Sylvia's salt-shaking rooster suddenly I do picture my mom showing me her new salt and pepper shakers—the dog and the cat—and making them bark and meow while we both filled them up, and I even remember when I broke the cat by accident and she was mad for a minute but then just shrugged and said, "Them's the breaks." And we both laughed.

Sylvia takes her hand from behind her back and shows me why she left the room. "Here, Milo. A present." She hands me a small square gift. It's flat and wrapped in flowery lady-type wrapping paper, which usually I'd hate but not this time. She tells me not to open it until later, and so that's what I do—in my bedroom after the supper that my sister ruined by telling us *in detail* how she dissected a cow's eye in biology, which did not add any flavor to my steak.

I usually just rip wrapping paper to shreds to get at the insides, but tonight I'm like a surgeon carefully removing the tape pieces so that I can preserve the sheet of gift paper "as is." Maybe I'll save it and use it to wrap a present I give to Summer. I stop for about half a second to realize I haven't thought much about Summer for a few days. But then the weight of whatever's inside the flowered paper calls me back to my task and I finish getting the last piece of tape off.

Peeling the paper back, I reveal the hidden treasure—the chocolate middle part of the Tootsie Pop. I stop wondering what Sylvia has given me when I see the thing that it is: It's an empty picture frame about the size of a playing card, and I know she removed a photo of her husband so that I can fill the frame again with someone I miss.

truce

I KNOW WHAT I HAVE TO DO.

I have to ask Marshall if he minds letting me cash in my half of the Freezie fund (equal to a grand total of $5.53). I don't tell him why and he doesn't ask, which is just Reason #47 why he's so great. Reason #48 is because right away he adds, "If you need it, take it all, Milo."

Next I need Hillary, and even though we haven't spoken since I blabbed all about her broken-doll box, I call her up and ask if we can meet somewhere. At first she says, "No way," but then she adds, "How about my front steps?" and I say, "I prefer neutral territory," so it's the Pit Stop where we decide to go to discuss what I want to do.

Because I get there first, I go ahead and buy her some gum—sort of as a peace offering and maybe as a bribe. It's sour watermelon gum, and it's her favorite, and she almost smiles when I hand it over.

We sit outside near the bike rack with our backs against the yellow cement wall. Because it's been sunny all morning, the wall is warm, and even through my flannel shirt, my back feels nice. She sits staring at the pack of gum and I just sit.

"It's okay," Hillary says, cutting me off. But she's not ready to look at me yet. Instead, she holds up the rectangle of packaged gum, and it looks like she's inspecting it for any flaws in the design. But then she digs around for the little piece of wrapper that you pull like a zipper that undoes the top, and she unwraps a piece of the pink-and-green gum and pops it in her mouth. I can smell the watermelon all the way from next to her, and it makes me smile because I hate the taste but love the smell.

"One more thing," I say, reaching in my coat pocket. And I watch her blow a perfect bubble as I pull my hand out and open it. "I found him."

It's the broken doll head and torso that I took home from her shoe box. As soon as the snow melted even a little, I started my rescue mission by spending different half hours digging around the row of bushes between our houses. When I finally spotted the crooked plastic shoulder sticking up through some dead leaves, I felt like I'd found a piece of me, and I actually gave him a bath in warm soapy water just to try to get the winter stains off.

I give the broken doll pieces back, and I can tell Hillary is being careful not to say anything that will make the whole good-talking part pop and so she only says, "Thanks, Milo."

She sits there thinking and holding the broken pieces in her hand, and I can tell she wants to say more, but secretly I'm glad that she doesn't.

"There's something else," I say. "Something I need help with."

"There's lots of things you need help with." And because she's smiling, I know this was actually a nice thing to say to me and that's exactly how I hear it.

"I want to go to yard sales and I need a guide," I tell her.

Hillary doesn't ask why I want to go to yard sales, but she does tilt her head the way I like. "What's going on in that brain of yours, Milo Cruikshank?"

And I smile back and say, "Secrets—the good kind. The kind that feel good."

Two teenagers walk up to the Pit Stop, and one of them has long black hair and the other one wears a ski hat even though it's April.

I make a note to throw out all my winter hats as soon as I get home.

windmills

IT FEELS LIKE FOREVER WAITING FOR THE weekend, but Hillary explains that no one has yard sales during the week, and even if they did, there's no way she'd skip school just to show me the ropes of buying cool stuff for cheap.

I just have to get through the week, which isn't so bad Monday through Thursday mainly because I get so busy with school and Mr. Shivnesky's tutoring and visits to Sylvia's that I forget about the plan. But Hillary calls me Thursday night and says, "Great news, Milo." And I'm honestly hoping her news has something to do with cake, but that's not why she calls. "I've gone through the *Penny-Pincher* with a highlighter, and there's going to be a ton of sales this weekend!"

The *Penny-Pincher* is this free newspaper you can pick up at the supermarket, and it's full of ads

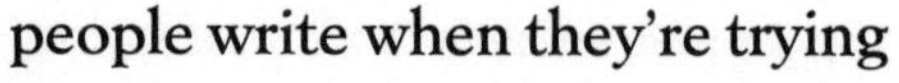

people write when they're trying to get rid of stuff or just want to wish their dog a happy birthday, which to be honest, just creeps me out.

I hang up excited that Saturday is almost

here but still wishing for some cake. All I have to do now is speed up Friday, but Friday is the worst because it's one of those school days that go really, *really* slow. Not even getting to watch part of a movie in Mrs. Favius's English class helps—mainly because it's a movie of Shakespeare's something or other that I can't understand because everyone talks so weird. As much as I think anything Mrs. Favius does is perfect, her Netflix list seems kind of lame.

Anyway, after English I have gym class, and there are no words to describe the way it feels to come in last when all you have to do is run laps around the stupid gym. This sounds pretty easy to do with the exception of it being twenty-five laps, which is like running to the Pit Stop and back home without getting to stop and buy a Freezie. What also makes the running harder is Mr. Thwaits, who thinks it's more "fun" to run while he throws dodge balls at you.

But after lunch the day is on cruise control. Science. Spanish. Health. These just seem to slip through my head, and before I realize it, the bell is ringing and my day is finally finished. I put a tiny check in the box that says School Week, pack up my books, and walk out the door a free man ready to meet tomorrow's yard sales head-on.

Saturday.

I'm up and dressed before the alarm that I set

for six forty-five because Hillary says success at yard sales is for the early birds. She says some people actually wait in their cars for the yard sale people to put out the tables and load them up and then they pounce on the yard sale. She also says it can get kind of ugly if the stuff being sold is cool junk and not just the junky kind.

My house is the meeting point, and my dad actually makes French toast for Marshall and me. Hillary says she's eaten already so just sits there while we wolf down the food. "Where are you kids off to?" my dad finally gets the courage to ask. I'm pretty sure he doesn't really want to know, but he asks because that's what a dad is supposed to do.

"School project," Hillary says before either Marshall or I could make something up. And I am impressed because I never told her not to talk about the plan—she just knew.

We're out the door and it's still just 7:30, so we make our first stop at the Pit Stop to stock up on the essentials—namely, one pack of candy or gum and one Freezie, because the budget is supposed to be for my yard sale search, not junk food.

"I've divided the neighborhood into three sections," Hillary says, spreading out a hand-drawn map that shows all the streets that are walkable to where we are. "Based on my experience, the best yard sales are on the green streets—those people love to get rid of stuff. I think they're possessed. The blue streets *might* be okay—because the *Penny-Pincher* said 'moving sale,' and moving people need to get rid of stuff. The yellow streets . . . I'd save them for last."

I am blown away by Hillary's color-coded map, and the thought in my head remembers that if it were last September, I'd think she was a freakish loser for making a map, let alone giving it color codes. But it's April, and the Me back then isn't the same Me who's walking side by side with two kids who are my friends. And a tiny voice in my brain whispers, *That's pretty cool.*

I'm wearing an empty cloth knapsack from the

basement, and it smells a little bit like moldy socks. I don't care. It's roomy enough for all sorts of stuff, and that's my mission: to fill it with things that remind me of stuff that was thrown away before the fog.

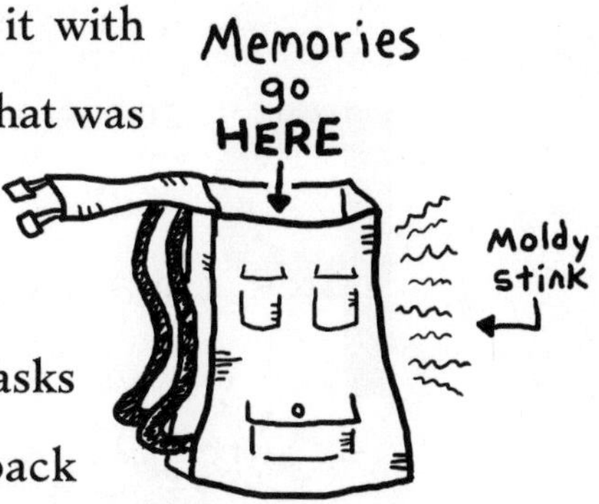

"You want to tell us what we're looking for?" Marshall asks as we pass the grape Freezie back and forth, and I'm shocked that Hillary actually takes a sip too and doesn't need her own germ-free straw, which I have in my pocket just in case.

"Nope." And I mean it. "I'm on a secret mission." And only Dabney St. Claire can truly appreciate the meaning of how secret missions need to be kept quiet, on a *need-to-know* basis. And right now no one needs to know anything but me.

It's not that I'm trying to be sneaky or stuck-up or something. It's just, how can I tell them what I'm looking for when I am not even sure what it is I need to find? I'm on a quest.

I'm just glad I'm not on my quest alone.

picking peas

PEOPLE WILL SELL ANYTHING THEY HAVE in their basements: the good, the bad, and the moldy.

It's clear pretty fast that some yard sales are like gold mines, while others are like a garbage truck just pulled up and dumped a load of junk on the front lawn. More than once Hillary has simply taken a look at the way the tables are laid out in the driveway and said, "Movin' on!"

I'm really happy I asked her to be our tour guide. It's almost eleven thirty in the morning so you know we're like pros by now. My knapsack is starting to fill up—not heavy, just bulky because when you're scouring for memories, they come in different shapes and sizes. I've spent only $4.50 and I think I'm doing pretty good. Marshall and Hillary have given up trying to guess what I'm up to, and now they're just off sorting through piles of one thing while I make my way through the musty boxes of something else.

"Hey, Milo," Marshall calls out from two tables away. "Check it out. Broken light sabers."

"Great," is all I can say, and I'm a little sorry

because there's Marshall holding up two plastic Star Wars light sabers and I'd really love to run over and have a Jedi duel with him, but I have to stay focused. I walk past a teetering stack of old records and then take a quick scan of a table laid out with mismatched dishes when I see something that makes my feet stick to the driveway tar.

I can't move forward—and I can't take my eyes off of the thing that's wedged between a trophy of a little guy fishing and a greasy popcorn popper. I finally move a little closer and see that, yes, it's a blanket. To anyone else it probably looks like just another ratty thing, but to me it's a time machine. Something inside me drops away like an out-of-control elevator and there's a blurry feeling in my brain as the fog swirls tight inside.

Just walk to it. Pick it up. Hold it. That's what I tell myself to do.

The touch is fuzzy and my body gets itchy with the memory of it. I pull it off the table and let the whole thing unfold until some of it is in my arms and the rest is on the driveway. The thing that floods me is that this blanket used to be in my house—sure, maybe it's not this exact one, but all that matters is this one looks the same. Dark green squares cover it, and within each square bright green dots have been lined up in rows and they stick up from the squares so that when you touch them, it's like how blind people read.

And as soon as I run my fingers along the straight rows of green dots, my whole body feels weird, and the next thing I know I have grabbed the blanket and run around the side of the house, where I hide beneath the weight of what used to be.

How many times had I seen this blanket on my mother's bed? How many naps had I taken beneath it? How could my dad get rid of such a perfect thing? I stare at the rows of dots—and then no matter how much I don't want it to happen, I cry.

I cry because I miss her. I cry because I can't ever stop feeling bad. . . .

"Milo?" It's Marshall and he's standing over me holding a Slinky that has been twisted and tangled so much, it will never walk down the stairs again. "Are you, you know . . . okay?"

First off, I feel awful that my best friend is seeing me crying and I make it seem like I'm not, which makes me cry some more. The One-Eyed Jack would never break apart in front of me, and now I feel like the balance of our whole friendship is ruined—all because of some stupid blanket.

"Yeah. I'm fine, Marsh," I barely say. "Just . . . allergies or something. The dust. You know."

I can tell he doesn't know.

So he does what I would do if the roles were reversed: He walks away.

Pull it together, I hear Dabney St. Claire's voice say inside my head. *No need to fall apart now.*

And though I'm used to his advice being great and stuff, this time his voice makes me tighten because it feels wrong. I can't be okay right now. I'm wrapped in a blanket that wants me to fall apart. This blanket was her blanket, and every other time I crawled into its warmth, she was there too, ready for me to let go of the nightmares or the bad days or just to be close. This blanket *is* her and now that I've found it (or one that is pretty much the same), the only thing I know to do is . . . let myself go.

Time is funny when you're lost in the fog, so I don't know if it's ten minutes or an hour that goes by. All I know for sure is that Hillary and Marshall slowly enter into where I'm staring, and they take their time sitting down next to me in the backyard of the yard sale house.

It's kind of like I sense their presence before I see them, and by the time I make eye contact, I see my two friends, who look at me without saying a word. And we just sit that way for a while—the three of us.

"That's a cool blanket," Hillary finally says, ignoring the part that I was just crying and there's some snot on it.

I nod.

"I like the bumps," Marshall adds. "Cool bumps."

I swallow the leftover crying stuff in my nose and then say, "I call them pea patches." Then I run a finger over the raised green dots. "See how each square is filled with exact rows of them? And they're totally the same color as peas."

"Actually . . ." I'm sure Hillary is about to say something about how peas aren't really that color or how they don't grow in patches, but I think the Dabney St. Claire in her head tells her to just keep quiet.

And even though it's a perfectly warm spring Saturday, I sit there wrapped tight in someone's tossed-out blanket surrounded by a knapsack of answers and two friends who keep their questions to themselves.

"In the hospital." I hear the sound of my voice before it becomes real. "In the hospital she got to have a blanket from home." Sitting there, I know I'm the one telling the story but I want to listen to it too, so I pay extra attention to my words as they spill out. "On her bed in the hospital. She had a blanket like this. Just like it."

I pull the corners tighter around my shoulders. "I don't remember how long she'd already been in the hospital. I just know my dad had us come with him, which we'd only done one time before, and it was actually a little fun because we got to order food from the cafeteria and watch a movie together sitting around her bed, and my mom was smiling a lot even when a nurse came in and asked us all to leave for five minutes so she could do something with a needle to her. . . . And I remember looking back as the nurse pulled the curtain that goes around the sickbed, and my mom made a goofy face at me right before the curtain cut off my view."

"Your mom was pretty silly, huh?" Hillary says this soft, like she isn't sure she should ask me anything.

But it's okay and I like being able to say, "Oh yeah. She was totally silly."

Still smiling, I stare down at all the peas on the blanket and then let the story out of me. "So it's a week later, and my dad has my sister and me come with him and I don't ask why, but right away this time it doesn't feel fun at all. This time the hospital smells bad, and all I see everywhere are empty wheelchairs and sick people stuck in those weird-shaped beds."

I close my eyes and picture that day, and it's so clear that I think I get the smell too—a mixture of cleaning stuff and something that will never smell good. "And I brought some flowers I picked in the backyard, which the nurse said she'd put inside some water for me but I'm not sure she ever did."

The images are all in my brain and I'm narrating the movie just like I'd do the play-by-play on a video game with Marshall, only this time there are no car crashes or alien spaceships—just me, my dad, and my sister standing in a moment stuck forever.

"So right before we go into her room, my dad bends down on a knee and I think he's going to comb back my hair or straighten my shirt, but he just gets down so he can look at my face and he says, 'Let's be brave, okay, little man?' And two things flash in my brain about what he says: 'be brave'—about *what*? Are we going to fight off zombie doctors to rescue Mom? And 'little man'? He never called me that before, and I remember how weird those words sounded. I was just this freaked-out kid standing in a stinky hospital wishing he could just wait in the car and play the radio as loud as he wants.

"But I was brave and I tried so hard to be a man, and then we walked into the room and I saw her surrounded by the pea-patch blanket. And she didn't see us yet and she wasn't smiling. She looked so sick, and as soon as she realized we were there, she tried to smile but I could tell she was faking it for us."

Marshall and Hillary just listen, and I'm listening too as I stare at the blanket—it's all I can see, and I'm staring so hard that I can make out the stitching and the individual fibers that wrap around my voice as I tell them what happened next.

"'Milo,' my mom said to me as I looked up at

her face. 'Milo. I'm going to be okay.' And I nodded, not sure what 'okay' really meant. 'I love you. No matter what. You know that, right?' And that's when I stopped looking at her. I couldn't look up and I couldn't say anything, and that was the last time I saw the blanket because that's when I found out she was going to have an operation to fix everything in her brain. And I guess we were there to wish her luck—but I felt stuck and frozen and didn't know what to do."

Right then I hear a car horn and then some kids laughing from the yard sale side of the house, which reminds me where I am. But I don't dare look away from the blanket to see Hillary's and Marshall's faces. The lump in my throat is growing, and I don't want to start crying again even though I can tell a few tears are already dripping down my face.

"If I knew that would be the last time I had to say anything to my mom, I would've said more. I would've said, 'I miss you.' I would've said, 'I love you.' I would've said, 'Please come home and make me supper and I don't care even if it's fish—I'll eat it and never complain again.' I would've climbed into that hospital bed with her and pulled the pea-patch blanket over both our heads and hugged her so tight. . . . But I couldn't do any of that. I just stood there silent and stared at the blanket that would always be hers."

There's total quiet for a full minute. I think I hear Hillary sniffle a little but don't try to look. Finally, it's Marshall who carefully speaks up.

"And then what happened?" he asks me—not to be a doofus, just because he cares.

But I don't answer him, and the three of us just sit there, and it isn't until later—when I'm home alone falling asleep on the couch—that I let the answer out of the tight little box I keep wrapped up in my gut. The answer is one I've kept hidden away, locked up and guarded so that I would never have to hear it or say it again.

I don't say it to Marshall. I don't say it to Hillary. I don't even say it to my dad. I say it to the blanket that's now wrapped around me.

"And then . . . ," I say out loud, listening carefully to each word. "And then she died."

"Sleep Tight"

things

MY DOOR IS CLOSED TIGHT.

I've spread all of my yard-sale treasures out on my bed on top of the pea-patch blanket.

These are the things I bought that remind me of her:

- Half bottle of red nail polish
- Glass swan with neck that's been glued back on
- Candy dish shaped like a leaf
- Lobster-claw pot holder
- Kitchen timer shaped like an egg
- Spray bottle of perfume with squeeze-bulb thingy
- Three plastic drink coasters with different seasons (Winter luckily is missing)
- Jewelry box with mismatched earrings and a cracked mirror inside
- Fuzzy blue bathrobe with one matching slipper
- Shampoo bottle that smells like summer vacation
- Sunglasses with big plastic frames
- Cat pepper shaker (different from the one I broke)

I stare at the things. I touch them. I close my eyes and imagine that each one really was my mom's.

With my eyes shut tight, I can hear her voice singing in the kitchen. Smells of the perfume she used to spray into the air drift toward me. And laughter—not just hers, but all of ours, plays like a song in the background. It's like a window somewhere is open and the fog inside lifts as fresh air blows into my brain.

But then . . .

"Milo, I—" My dad walks into my room. My eyes pop open and the magic feeling inside disappears and is instantly replaced by the fog. Whoosh.

My dad stares at my bed and all of the things I've placed there. I stop breathing.

"What is all this?" he asks me in a tone that does not sound promising. I try to block his view with my body, which is just a silly attempt on my part.

"Stuff," I say. "Just stuff." I can't tell him the truth. I'm so scared he'll want to throw it all away like he did before.

But he is already walking around me and he kneels on my floor, and I am shocked to watch him reach out and touch the old blanket I found. He runs his fingers over the peas.

"Dad?"

He picks up the candy dish. He touches the

swan. He touches the fabric of the ratty bathrobe.

"Milo, where did all of this come from?" He sounds worried somehow, and of course I assume I am in the biggest trouble ever.

Between a fabulous lie and the truth, I choose the true part because I can't think of anything that would sound even a little believable. "Yard sales. With Hillary and Marshall. I bought stuff that made me think of her. Of Mom." The words tumble out hard.

And a strange thing happens. He doesn't ask why or pick up the phone and have me committed to a hospital where doctors will ask me questions about being crazy. My father, my dad, just nods his head, and I watch the slow way it bobs up and down—almost automatic like a robot. Then he opens his arms, and the next thing I know, I am buried in him and falling deep inside his shirt and I'm crying so hard I hardly notice his tears are making my head wet too.

The smallest breeze blows through my mind—a window somewhere is open just a crack, and the fog knows enough to leave us both alone.

the grin truth

IT'S AFTER SCHOOL AND IT'S NOT A MR. Shivnesky Monday or Thursday, but still I am waiting around outside because my dad is swinging by to pick me up so we can go to the orthodontist.

Apparently, my teeth, which no one was paying attention to while my mom was dead, have kind of gone their separate ways and finally it's time to rein them in before they migrate into someone else's mouth.

My friends keep me company while I wait, and both give me pep talks from their own personal experiences, which is way better than the lame advice my father (who has never had a cavity in his life) gave me: "Braces are cool, Milo. You'll see." Braces are *cool*? Where do parents learn to say such dumb stuff?

"Really, Milo, braces aren't so bad," Hillary says, showing off her wireless teeth without meaning to. "I mean, sure there's the pain every time they get tightened and the constant brushing and flossing part. Oh, and you get used to not being able to have popcorn or gum or chewy candy. But in the end, when you see the difference they make, it is so worth the work!"

"*Work?* Braces are work?" Now I am totally bummed because I was picturing braces as being much more like some sort of accessory they simply attach to you, like a bionic arm that you just use without any fuss.

Next up is Marshall. "First things first. Forget everything Miss Perfect just said. Here's the real deal. You eat what you want. Brush when you can. And flossing? Like, that's just not gonna happen."

Marshall says all this as upbeat as ever, but as he talks, I notice a huge piece of some gross green food thing lodged in his wires, and I imagine it has probably been stuck there since the day I met him eight months ago! I strain to figure out what it is, which is maybe a piece of a lime jelly bean or perhaps lettuce from an ancient taco. His mouth keeps flapping away but I don't hear him because I can't stop staring at this *thing*, and even when I look away for a second, there it is staring back at me like some alien being living in his mouth

Inside Marshall's Mouth

and I get the thought that it's possible that piece of food is controlling Marshall's brain! And if you knew Marshall, you'd agree that maybe that would explain everything!

The car horn beeps. It's my dad and I am so dreading this. Marshall stands and salutes me; Hillary just waves and mouths the word "bye," and I can't help but notice how nice her teeth look.

Dr. Veerlawn's office is downtown inside one of those old office buildings that's chock-full of other doctor types. It's just a first visit to assess the dental damage, but still I'm a bit on the nervous side. I relax a little when I open the glass door with Dr. Veerlawn's name on it because the first thing I see in the waiting room is a PlayStation so I know this guy is going to be cool—even if it's his job to twist my teeth with huge pliers.

"Milo Cruikshank," I announce to the lady behind the check-in desk, who I notice is wearing braces even though she is a *grown-up*. This kind of creeps me out, so I go play a video game and wait for my dad to finish parking the car.

I am too busy trying to keep my race car from sliding off the muddy track to pay attention to the annoying voice that enters the office.

"Mom. Mom. *Mo-ther!* . . . I am not being stubborn. I'll call you as soon as I'm done. . . . Yes! Right after. Ugh!"

My car, an orange dune buggy with massive wheels, hits a rock the size of Peru and I am engulfed in flames as pieces of the buggy fly at the screen in super slo-mo.

"Next time try the blue dragster. It has less suspension but handles the curves better."

I turn to face the annoying voice, but when I do, I am surprised to see that it belongs to Summer Goodman, who is in my new orthodontist's office. She's sitting in the chair next to me, and I watch as she reaches into her purse and takes out a sparkly pink plastic case. "Oh, thanks for the tip," I say, trying hard not to gawk at her.

"I've played that thing a million times." She

opens the sparkly case and takes out a purple retainer and pops it into her mouth as simple as if it were a breath mint, which frankly I wish I had right now. "You get really good if your teeth are bad enough. Trust me. First time here?"

I want to answer but am too caught up in noticing that with her retainer in her mouth Summer talks with a *tiny* lisp, so "First time here" sounds like "Firthst time here."

"Uh, yeah. My teeth kind of need help." And as proof, I actually open my mouth wide so that she can witness the scattered lineup inside.

"Whoa. You are gonna get top thcore with that meth."

We both laugh, which I can't quite believe. It's the most normal thing that's ever happened between us—not that much has happened at all.

She keeps talking. "Veerlawn ith gonna love thothe." She is now pointing at my mismatched mess of a mouth.

"I'm glad I can help the guy out." I laugh again. "Um . . . when did yours come off?"

She's using her tongue to slip the retainer on and off her teeth like she's done it a hundred times. I can tell she doesn't even realize she does it. It makes her look much younger. "Latht thummer. Right before thchool thtarted. And you want to know the very firtht thing I did? Went to the Pit Thtop and bought a pack of Thtrawberry Thquirt gum. Chewed the whole pack before I even got home. Mmmm . . . I can thtill tathte it!"

She grabs the second controller and expertly navigates the menu to set the game up for two players. She's already picked the blue drag racer, so I go for a motorcycle with a sidecar. "It'th your funeral," she says, seeing my choice.

We're midway around the second lap, and she is by far the better racer, when a man in a blue doctor costume pokes his head around the corner and says, "Okay, Summer. You're up."

She doesn't hit pause. Instead, she drives her car directly off the cliff so that it explodes in midair. And then she gets up, turns to me, and grins. "Crash and burn. I love that part. Thee ya, Milo."

"Yeah," I say, kind of stunned by too many things all at once. "See ya, Summer."

She leaves just as my dad walks in. Apparently, the parking lot has way too many floors, and it took him a while to navigate the maze of doors to get out of the place. "Who was that?" he asks as Summer disappears into one of the many little rooms off the hallway. "Friend of yours?"

And there are so many ways I would've answered that question this past year. But the answer is actually pretty simple, and it's what I tell my dad: "Just some kid from school," I say, and I don't need Dabney St. Claire or anyone else to tell me that it's one more thing that's getting straightened out.

digging in the dirt

"MULCH!"

Marshall is zigzagging between the rows of plants that line the outdoor part of the Green Scene. "I love that word. Say it—your mouth has to chuckle. Mulch!"

Hillary just shrugs and adjusts her cupped hands that are full of tulip bulbs.

"You're nuts, Marshall. Certifiable."

"Mulch!"

We are at the Green Scene with Sylvia, who came to get some flowers—gladiolas, I think—and asked if we wanted to come along. We'd been sitting on my front steps trying to name the best Life Savers flavors (top five: Spear-O-Mint, Tropicals, Tangy Fruits, Wild Cherry, Wint-O-Green), and all it took was a nod of our heads and we were in.

"Planting spring flowers makes me smile," Sylvia told us while we drove to the greenhouse that's near the highway. "And I just love when the dirt gets wedged under my fingernails and I can't get it out for days."

I look through a catalog of different plants and flowers and talk to the guy who works there. I'm trying to find the name of a plant that used to be outside House #3—it's one my mom loved when it bloomed. "It was yellow," I tell the guy whose name tag says LEO.

"More like a tree or more like a bush?" Leo asks.

He's flipping pages of the book that shows pictures of what has to be every growing thing on the planet. We're like detectives trying to narrow down our suspects.

"A bush. It grew all over the backyard, and the flower part was small—kind of like an opened-up banana peel."

This new information must mean something because Leo gets that "aha" look and flips some more pages in the book. "Like this?" Proud-like, he turns the book to face me.

"Yes!" I say. "That's the one. Exactly."

"Forsythia," Leo says. "Early to bloom. Easy to grow. Very popular."

I laugh a little because I always thought my mom was saying "for Cynthia," like she was visiting a girl secretly buried in our backyard every time she went to take care of the plant.

"Forsythia." I say it out loud and then go with Leo to look at the ones you can buy.

Later it's just Sylvia and me standing in my backyard, and she's got her shovels and some soil in a small wheelbarrow from her garage. "Nice idea, Milo." Sylvia is all gung ho about planting my mom's favorite bush.

"The way I see it, every time they bloom, I'll think of her." I start digging the hole where the small bush will go. The ground is harder than I thought and it takes some effort to get past the rocks and roots, but ten minutes later Sylvia says I've dug deep enough.

She's a pro at this so she has me place the plant's butt inside the narrow hole, and then I use the small spade to shovel in clumps of new dirt, burying the roots of the plant all the way to the top.

"I bet she'd really love this," I say. "Thanks for helping."

"My pleasure," Sylvia says. And then after a few seconds go by, she adds, "You know, Milo, remembering your mother any way you can is really important. But there's something else too."

"What's that?" I ask, sort of aware that I'm not sure I want to know the answer. We're patting the new dirt down around the base of the forsythia and our hands are touching.

"After Paul died, the memory of him was all I had. He was all I thought about, and all I did was miss him in a sad and lonely kind of way."

"But you still think about him all the time. All those pictures. The stories."

She smiles. "Yes. Now those are good memories.

But I had to make room for them because the sad ones were taking up all the space."

I watch as her hands scoop up one more pile of dirt and add it to the base of the plant. "It's what saying good-bye is all about, Milo. It's making room for the good memories to spread and take root—like the bush."

"But I have good memories. Now I do, anyway."

And it's true, thanks to all the great yard-sale stuff I've collected. But she is right about one thing.

"I never did say good-bye. It all happened so fast, and then it was just . . . over." I am suddenly uncomfortable and just want to go watch TV.

"Maybe while you finish planting the forsythia it would be a perfect time to say it. Good-bye, I mean."

Sitting in the dirt, I let Sylvia talk and I just listen. She asks if I want to imagine the last time I saw my mother so I can picture her and picture me and use that picture to actually have me say "good-bye" to my mother. "You don't have to," Sylvia says. "It's just an idea."

I glance down at the skinny forsythia stems sticking out of the dirt like twisted fingers. "Okay," I say, though I'm not 100 percent sure.

But I take a deep breath and close my eyes and go backward to that last time I saw my mom, and this is a secret place I have kept tucked way back on the highest shelf inside me. It's a place I never wanted to see again, but Sylvia's hand on my shoulder helps me push hard, and I let myself open the memory of the hospital and I fill up on the sick smells that make my nose burn and let the sound of soft nurse shoes scurrying down the hallway come back to me.

All I can do is stare at the floor that is dull green linoleum because I am scared all over. I don't want to be back in this room, in this memory, but deep inside I know it's something I have to do. . . .

...and when I slowly look up- what I see is **ME** looking small and frightened.

And there's my sister and my father...
We all stand next to a hospital bed laid **FLAT.**

And my **MOTHER** is here but she is asleep- ready for the operation that promises to hit the **RESET** button of our lives.

Her eyes are closed and her **SMILE** has already been erased...
Her head has been **SHAVED** and it's shiny- very shiny except for the faint blue lines that make a landing strip on top.

N
W
E
S
These are the lines that will guide the Doctors on their **TREASURE HUNT** to save my MOM.

The thought that her head will be **CUT OPEN** runs away from me...
and to feel **SAFE** I picture how those lines make a Tic-Tac-Toe board on my mother's head.

X.O.X. Kisses and hugs.

My father puts a hand on my head and another one on my sister's. That's the cue that we have to go, and the reality dawns on me—we have been brought there to say good-bye because it's impossible to know what will happen when they operate, and I am terrified to say a single word because that would be admitting the possibility of something I could never accept.

"It's time," a nurse says, and then I am walking away from the last time I will ever be loved again.

And I freeze inside and want to say something to her—but no words exist.

A final look back and people in dull gray gowns and white masks are already swarming around her and I picture crows pecking and poking and I have to look away but there's no place to look that doesn't feel and smell like a hospital.

And that's when the fog settles inside me for the first time and I just let it fill me all the way up because it's so nice to let my feelings get wrapped up in thick blankets that will be stored away somewhere safe.

My eyes open. Sylvia sits cross-legged in the dirt beside me and she watches me, but I don't feel like being looked at. I don't feel like much at all.

"This is stupid," I say to her. "It's just a dumb bush."

Sylvia tries to put her hand back on my shoulder, but I just move like I have to pick up the shovel. "Thanks for helping," I tell her, and she's smart enough to know that means it's time to leave.

I go back in my house, mad at myself for letting Sylvia talk me into remembering the hospital. I don't need to say good-bye. And to prove it, I just stare out my bedroom window at the forsythia we planted . . . and watch as the twilight sneaks up and makes it disappear into the night.

tuna fish

I CAN'T SLEEP.

I'm still tangled in the memory mess left over from what I remembered this afternoon. The frightening moments before her operation, before she died, are always freeze-framed pictures that make me want to shrink and hide.

Lying in bed staring at the ceiling, I just want to get out of the house, and so even though it's past midnight, I grab a sweatshirt and take my flashlight and wander out to the backyard. Shining the beam onto the forsythia, I smile at the hints of yellow that are already waving at me.

When I turn the flashlight off, I am blown away by how many stars are in the sky. I lie on my back and just stare up at the sky, trying to put together the easy constellations, which, to be honest, look like big games of connect-the-dots.

Do I fall asleep? I'm not sure. But in the stars my mom's face is lit up by hundreds of connected dots, and then my face fills in next to her. And she isn't sick. And I'm not sad. And I realize I can say good-bye any way I want to.

She is so pretty in the sky, and together we dance between the seconds that my heart beats under my sweatshirt. I don't have to hang on to the sick image of her and let that be my good-bye. I decide this is the face I will hold on to, and then shooting stars are all that I see as I let the words skip out of my lips.

"Tuna fish, Mom."

And her smile lights up my wet eyes. "Tuna fish."

growth spurt

IT'S A FAST-FORWARD DAY—WHERE THE MINUTES just whiz by.

It starts with the car ride to school, which my dad *offers* even though I don't have Cheerios. After dropping my sister off at the high school, the rest of the drive together goes by so fast that I don't even think about needing the Top 5 Topics to help me survive.

"Mr. Shivnesky says you're doing pretty good," my dad says between stoplights on Highland Street. And then quickly he adds, "But he still wants to see you after school."

"I know," I say. "I actually sort of like going. But don't ever repeat that out loud, okay?"

"Way to go, kiddo," he says, and even though I hate the word "kiddo," I know he's said something nice, which is cool.

"Truth is, I probably won't end up one of those NASA guys who has to use math to save a space shuttle or anything, but I'm pretty sure I won't flunk. That's what Mr. Shivnesky tells me, anyway."

My dad nods and then a big grin swallows his face. "Hey, what's with that guy's head? Does he shave it or what?"

We both laugh while some oldie comes on the radio about a girl named Alison. The song makes my dad tap the inside knuckles of his fingers against the steering wheel like he used to do on our family trips. It's an old habit I haven't seen in a long time, and I can tell his tapping makes a different noise now, which at first I think is because it's a different car—but then I see the real reason: He doesn't wear a wedding ring anymore. The ring was what made the tap-tap-tapping crisp and real—and it's the only time a piece of fog threatens to invade the car ride.

But then we're at school already. And I'm off with a quick wave and a toot of the horn. Take that, fog!

Gym is just a joke. We're supposed to do the fifty-yard dash while Mr. Thwaits times us, but what I really think he's doing is using mind control

to see who he can make trip and fall flat on their face so that everyone else can laugh.

"Yo, Milo." Hillary catches up to me after I come out of the office, where the school nurse, who is really the secretary named Mrs. Cranston, has checked me out for broken bones. Nothing's busted—or so I'm told.

Hillary and I walk toward the cafeteria. She smells nice, which I don't tell her. And she drops her favorite pen, which I do. "You don't want to lose this," I say, handing over the chewed-up Bic with the green cap.

"It's like Excalibur to me," she says, and then chews the tip out of habit, which makes me smile, and not even the smell of the cafeteria's spaghetti and meatballs gets in the way.

"Dude," Marshall says later while we try to open his locker, which has been sticking lately due mainly to the fact that Mark Tompkins poured some sort of glue in the hinges. "I tried calling you last night. I found a major spoiler online for *Countdown to Zero*."

Countdown to Zero is this sci-fi flick about alien tracker droids who might really be made with human DNA, which is probably the reason they like hanging around malls and eating people. It's coming out this summer, and Marshall has become *totally* obsessed with knowing every single thing about it—even the surprise ending, which I told him not to tell me unless it's really awesome.

"Sorry," I say. "I was out with my dad." I pause and then tell the rest. "Bowling. He took me bowling."

Marshall's face shows exactly what it was like. Weird. But I got a strike and ate two hot dogs and got to watch my dad throw a ball in the wrong lane by mistake, and we both cringed when it hit the metal pin protector thing—really loud! And then the guy who sprays the stinky shoes got really mad and told us to next time try the Super Bowl down the street.

"It was actually kind of fun."

Marshall gives me the thumbs-up sign, which means he thinks so too.

"Oh, and he wants to know if you want to come over Sunday and go to a movie or something."

"No can do," Marshall tells me while we walk down the crowded hall. "Sunday is—" He stops like he's just realized the next step is a cliff. "Can't do it." That's all he says.

The bell rings and it's math class, so I just say, "Whatever" and high-five Marshall before walking into my classroom.

It isn't until after school when I look at the calendar hanging on the kitchen door that I instantly see what kept Marshall's sentence from taking that next step.

Sunday is Mother's Day.

franken-mom

I TELL MYSELF THAT JUST BECAUSE SHE ISN'T here doesn't mean I don't have a mother. The last two Mother's Days were just skipped over, deleted from the playlist, and going to a movie or simply ignoring the day won't work for me.

On Mother's Day restaurants fill up with all the Queens of the World. We order pizza and watch the news.

Two years ago was the worst. That was the first year she was gone, when my fifth-grade art teacher thought we should waste valuable class time to make our mothers something "special." Brian Kelley made an ashtray (I guess his mother smoked, and I wondered why he would want to celebrate that). Elana McEnroe used plastic bottles to make wind chimes, which pretty much made the dullest noise I ever heard. There were a couple of mosaics that spelled HAPPY MOTHER'S DAY and a few different fiascoes of a clay figurine meant to hold a heart or flowers, but it really doesn't matter what they were supposed to hold because those things just break off when the clay dries.

Then there was me. And I felt so awful, I just filled a piece of paper with lines that crissed and crossed back and forth over and under each other until the whole sheet was just darkness with the smallest pieces of light sticking through.

It's moments like those—when the flashlight shines on all the ways mothers exist—that I shrivel up inside. Dabney St. Claire says that's because I'm still hurting. "Duh," I say back to him. "Of course I'm hurting!"

I've watched kids getting their foreheads kissed and kids being yelled at inside their cars, and every time I wish I were the kid who still had the mom, no matter how mean or sad or angry she might be. That mom is better than no mom, though my mom is who I miss most.

"Good morning," I say to my sister, who is almost as shocked as I am that I am standing at the foot of her bed at one o'clock on a Saturday afternoon. "Family meeting. Ten minutes." And I walk out before she can start in on me. I mean business.

My dad is completely absorbed watching a baseball game on TV, but he mutes it as soon as I stand in front of his view. "We're having a family meeting in the kitchen. Your presence is required." And that's all I say, though I do grab the remote and put the sound back on for him.

"Milo?" I hear him call after me.

"Kitchen. Ten minutes." That's all I say back.

I make some chocolate milk and lay out a plate of Oreos and am pretty much surprised they both actually show up.

"What's up with you?" my sister says. She stands by the sink with her arms crossed. My dad unscrews an Oreo so he can scrape off the cream with his teeth. I had no idea grown-ups even knew about that.

"The floor is yours, Milo. Go for it."

I start by saying, "Thanks for showing up on such short notice." And then after my dad grabs three Oreos at once, I add, “Two cookies to a customer.”

“Hurry it up,” my sister says. “I got stuff to do.”

By “stuff,” she means “nothing,” but I want this over with as fast as possible too, so I just blurt it all out.

“I want to have Mother’s Day.”

“Oh, please,” my sister moans.

My dad just picks cookie out of his teeth. The clock ticks and the TV tells us the baseball score from the living room, but we don’t speak. Finally, my dad shocks us all by saying, “I think that’s a great idea, Milo. A really great idea.”

And then my sister shrugs and says the most surprising thing yet. “Yeah, fine. What do you want?”

And with both of them in on the idea, I drop the bomb I’ve been carrying around inside me for a while.

“I want to bring Mom back to life.”

mother's day

ONCE UPON A TIME THERE WAS A box in the attic. Sealed up with tons of tape, the box was banished and forgotten about and just sat there gathering dust in the darkness and the fog. But now my dad has climbed the shaky ladder and hands down the cardboard box that is surprisingly light to be holding so many heavy feelings.

Family pictures are going back on the wall, and even my sister helps slide a few of the old photos into the yard sale frames I bought. My dad holds the hammer and helps bang in picture hooks, but after doing two or three, he looks down at me and I'm afraid he's just giving up or remembering he'd rather be filling in the squares of his crossword puzzles. But that's not the reason.

"I think you can take it from here, okay, Milo?"

And you know what? It is okay. Because he isn't saying that so he can disappear. He is saying it so he can dig into the box of pictures that he now helps unpack. He's keeping me company while I bring my mom back from the dead.

"Look, you and Mom making a snowman!" he says. "It was that huge storm . . . I took this one in my bathrobe."

And then I hear music coming from the kitchen, and a few pots and pans bang and clang while I hammer nails in the wall, and soon the house fills with the smells of something cooking, and then my dad carries out a huge tray of plates and syrup and orange juice while my sister holds a steaming stack of blueberry pancakes. "I used the frozen blueberries, but still, I think they'll taste okay." My sister is actually smiling.

And that's where we celebrate Mother's Day—sitting on the floor against the wall in the living room. And for the first time in a long time, there's noise and smells and pictures in the house, and in between bites of pancakes—where the blueberries taste great—I'm happy to be a family of three, remembering we once were four.

phantom smiles

SHE WAS—

A pirate

A princess

A dancer

A dreamer

A nurse

A magician

A chef

A friend

A hole I thought could never be filled

She is—

Alive again

The pea-patch blanket drapes across the couch, so whenever we watch TV, she does too.

A silly apron hangs by the stove on a hook, watching over meals and offering silent cooking tips.

A crooked line of photographs hangs on walls that watch me walk by—her smile always there to remind me she is close even though she can't be.

And by my bed the picture frame Sylvia gave me can barely contain the image of my mom and me reaching for the sky every single day.

Acknowledgments

TELLING MILO'S STORY WOULD'VE BEEN impossible if not for the friends and family members who have held me close over the years. Thank you all.

Thank you to the James Thurber House for their generous support and attic apartment, where I had time and space to finish writing and cartooning the book. Thanks to my agent, Jill Grinberg, for believing in my story from the start and for getting it in the hands of the amazing Liesa Abrams, who nurtured and guided me through the editing process with bottomless respect and encouragement. Art director extraordinaire Karin Paprocki embraced my squiggly lines and created the wonderful visual design of the book. Go Team Milo!

Finally, Milo would still be lost in the fog if not for the support and love of my wife, Kalie, and my son, Zach, who make every day complete.